THE FAMOUS FIVE AND
THE MISSING CHEETAH

THE FAMOUS FIVE are Julian, Dick, George (Georgina by rights), Anne and Timmy the dog.

Arriving for two weeks' stay at Big Hollow, the children are delighted to discover that Tinker has a new friend – a cheetah!

But twenty-four hours' later, Attila the cheetah has been kidnapped, and his abductors threaten to shoot him unless they're given the formula for a new, top-secret fuel.

Cover illustration by John Cooper

Also available in Knight Books:

The Famous Five and the Missing Cheetah

A new adventure of the
characters created by
Enid Blyton, told by Claude
Voilier, translated by
Anthea Bell

Illustrated by John Cooper

KNIGHT BOOKS
Hodder and Stoughton

Copyright © Librairie Hachette 1972
First published in France as *Les Cinq au Cap des Tempetes*
English language translation copyright ©
Hodder and Stoughton Ltd. 1981
Illustrations copyright © Hodder and
Stoughton Ltd. 1981

First published in Great Britain by
Knight Books 1981
Fourth impression 1984

British Library C.I.P.

Voilier, Claude
    The Famous Five and the missing cheetah.
    I. Title
    843'.914[J]   PZ7

    ISBN 0-340-27248-1

Printed and bound in Great Britain for
Hodder and Stoughton Paperbacks, a
division of Hodder and Stoughton Ltd.,
Mill Road, Dunton Green, Sevenoaks,
Kent (Editorial Office: 47 Bedford
Square, London, WC1 3DP) by
Hunt Barnard Printing Ltd.,
Aylesbury, Bucks.

CONTENTS

Chapter One

OFF TO BIG HOLLOW!

'Here you are, Dick – the piece of string you wanted! Catch! You can tie that bundle of clothes to the carrier of your bike now – though it won't look very elegant! Oh, Anne – fancy trying to get so much into one suitcase! It's *never* going to shut! For goodness' sake, Timmy! Do *try* not to get underfoot the whole time! How do you think we're ever going to be ready?'

'Stop grumbling, George!' said Julian, laughing. 'Aren't you pleased we're off at last?'

'Well, of course! You know I am!'

George closed a little duffle bag she had just finished packing, and grinned at her cousin.

'I may be talking an awful lot, Ju, but that's just because I'm so happy! Do you realise – we're actually going to have a whole fortnight with Tinker and Mischief at Big Hollow! What a lovely, exciting change in the middle of our summer holidays at Kirrin Cottage. It's a real stroke of luck the Haylings invited us – oh, I do wish we were already there!'

Uncle Quentin and Aunt Fanny, George's mother and father, lived at Kirrin Cottage, and they always asked their two nephews and their niece to stay in the summer holidays. Julian was the eldest of the children. Then came Dick, and then his cousin George, who looked a little like Dick because they both had short, dark hair. Julian and Dick's sister Anne was the youngest of the four cousins.

George was an only child. She wished very much she had been born a boy, and her cousins knew by now that she simply hated to be called by her real name, Georgina!

All four children got on very well with each other – and with George's beloved dog Timmy. Timmy, George's inseparable companion, was the fifth of the Five!

Just now, the four children were busy loading up the carriers of the fine new bicycles Uncle Quentin had given them. They were all looking forward to their two weeks at Big Hollow House. The house belonged to Professor Hayling, a famous scientist and a great friend of Uncle Quentin, who lived there with his son Tinker.

'Big Hollow's not very far from Kirrin,' said Dick. 'It won't take us long to get there.'

'I love Big Hollow!' George said. 'From the upstairs windows, you can see right across to the sea and Tinker's lighthouse on Demon's Rocks!'

'Poor Tinker!' said Anne. 'Not having a mother, he must get very bored all by himself in the hols, with Professor Hayling so wrapped up in his work the whole time!'

'Well, we'll all do our best to amuse him!' said Julian cheerfully. 'I bet he's pleased we're coming to stay!'

'Everybody ready?' asked Dick. He had finished tying a big bundle of clothes to the back of his bike.

'We've been ready for *ages*!' said George. She was already mounting her own bicycle. 'I do think it was splendid of Father to give us these grand new bikes to replace our old ones.'

'Yes,' said Julian, getting on his own bicycle too. 'It was a really wonderful present from Uncle Quentin. Goodbye, Aunt Fanny – we'll send you lots of postcards!'

The children gave Aunt Fanny a last wave, and set off along the road. Timmy was running along beside George's bike as usual. He loved it when he got a chance to stretch his legs!

'I bet Tinker will come to meet us!' said Anne. The wind was ruffling her fair hair as they rode along.

'Oh yes, I'm sure he will,' said George. 'He *does* get rather bored, all on his own. Professor Hayling is so absorbed in his inventions and all his rows and rows of figures that he has hardly any time to spare for poor Tinker.'

'I like old Tinker!' announced Dick, pedalling hard to get a good start up a rather steep hill. 'And I bet you'll be pleased to see your friend Mischief again, Timmy!'

'Woof!' said Timmy, running as fast as ever.

The Five left Kirrin behind them, passed the village of Little Hollow, where they noticed new signs pointing to a zoo, and came to the village of Big Hollow. When they were past Big Hollow village too, George suddenly shouted out, 'Tinker! Here comes Tinker!'

'Oh, look – he's got Mischief on his shoulder!' said Anne happily.

A boy with a funny little monkey clinging to his shoulder was riding towards them on a very creaky, rusty old bike. When he had come up to them he stopped.

'Hallo, everyone!' he cried cheerfully. 'My word, it's good to be together again!'

They all got off their bikes and greeted one another – even Mischief, who solemnly shook paws with Timmy! Then the five children set off again, riding towards Big Hollow House. When they came round to the last bend in the road, they could see Demon's Rocks village ahead, and the lighthouse just off the coast. It really was Tinker's very own lighthouse. His father had once bought it when he needed absolute peace and quiet for some very important work, and when he had finished with it he gave it to Tinker. Tinker used to have wonderful games there, and he and the Five had once had a big adventure while they were spending a few days in the lighthouse. Last time the Five stayed with the Haylings, however, they hadn't been able to use the lighthouse because it was thought to have been damaged in a storm.

'What a shame we can't sleep in it this time!' said George.

'Actually it's not as badly damaged as my dad

thought at first,' said Tinker. 'He asked an architect to look over it, and the architect said it was quite all right for playing in – but I think it would hurt old Jenny's feelings if we slept there this time!'

Anne was secretly rather glad they were sleeping at the house – she'd been frightened when there had been a big storm once, while all the children were staying in the lighthouse!

'Well, I'm glad it's safe to play there, anyway,' said Julian. 'We can go over in your boat *Bobabout*! and have some grand games, Tinker!'

'Yes, and we can go to the new zoo at Little Hollow,' said Tinker.

'Ooooh yes,' said Dick.

'Look – here's Big Hollow!' said Julian, as they approached the Haylings' house, which had the same name as the nearby village. Tinker got off his bike.

'I've got a big surprise for you,' he told the others, with a gleam in his eye. 'But I'm not going to tell you what it is! You'll soon see, once you get through the gate – so watch out!'

The little boy opened the big heavy gate, inviting his friends to follow him in. They did, wondering what sort of surprise Tinker could have for them. Suddenly, Anne let out a cry of alarm – and she was answered by the growl of a wild animal!

A huge, catlike creature had bounded out on to the garden path!

'Don't worry,' Tinker calmly told the Five, who were staring at the big cat in amazement.

'Attila isn't at all ferocious! A friend of my father's – he's an explorer – brought him back from Africa, and when he'd tamed him, he gave him to us as a present. He makes a wonderful watchdog! Here, Attila! Come here, boy!'

Timid Anne pressed close to her elder brother. Julian, Dick and George, very interested, looked at the big animal. He really did look like a huge cat with bright yellow fur and black spots.

'He – he's like a lion, or a tiger, or a leopard!' stammered poor Anne.

'Well, he isn't any of those – he's a cheetah!' Tinker explained. 'Though *I* think he's more like a great big dog disguised as a cat! Attila wouldn't hurt a soul – unless it was someone trying to get in and burgle our house. Well, Tim, old boy, what do *you* think of him?'

Timmy was puzzled! He looked suspiciously at the cheetah. But when he saw little Mischief spring fearlessly up on the big cat's back, he came a little closer. Attila took a couple of steps forward too. There was a moment of suspense – and then, at exactly the same time, the two animals stretched their necks and began sniffing each other.

'Woof!' said Timmy, in a friendly way.

And Attila began purring. He sounded like a big spinning top humming! Mischief seemed to realise that the other two animals had made friends, because he began to clap his hands and jump for joy!

George burst out laughing, and so did the

others. They weren't in the least afraid of the cheetah now!

Hearing them all in the garden, Jenny, the Haylings' housekeeper, came out. She was a plump, busy little woman, who looked after Tinker and his father. She was very fond of Tinker, and the boy liked her too.

'Oh, there you are, children!' said Jenny. 'Come along in. I do hope Attila didn't frighten you! Goodness knows why they gave him such a fierce sort of name – even without a muzzle on, he's as gentle as a kitten!'

Anne wasn't sure that she entirely believed Jenny, but she didn't say so. Tinker took the Five off to the Professor's study to say hallo. The Professor was hard at work, as usual.

'Here they are, Dad! They've just arrived,' Tinker said.

'*Who's* just arrived? I didn't invite anyone!' said the scientist.

'Yes, you did, Dad! Don't you remember? You invited George and Dick and Julian and Anne to stay!'

'Good morning, Professor Hayling!' said the children, in chorus.

'Oh, good morning, good morning … my regards to your father, George! Do come and see me again one of these days, won't you?'

'Dad, they *have* come to see you!' said Tinker. 'They've come to *stay* – for a fortnight! You *can't* have forgotten!'

'Stay for a fortnight, Tinker? *Who's* staying for a fortnight? Oh, do move away from that

14

window, boy, you're blocking the daylight! And what's that dog doing here? You'd better tell Attila to chase it away! Why are people always interrupting my work? Dogs, indeed – they're always full of fleas!'

'No, listen, Dad, this is Timmy! George's dog! You *know* Timmy – you're friends with him!'

'Full of fleas, that's what they are!' the Professor grumbled to himself.

And forgetting all about the children, he went back to looking at his papers with their rows and rows of figures.

Chapter Two

WHERE IS ATTILA?

Tinker led his friends out of the study again. George was bursting with fury.

'Fancy saying poor Timmy was full of fleas! How *could* he be so unfair? Honestly, your father's gone too far this time, Tinker! I'm going straight home to Kirrin Cottage – I'm not staying another minute!'

Tinker and her cousins had quite a job to calm her down! But at last she said all right, she'd agree to stay at the Haylings' house.

Out in the garden, the cheetah was playing with Mischief and Jenny was watching them.

'Everyone here loves Attila,' said Tinker proudly. 'Jenny does, and I do, and Mischief does – and even Dad remembers he exists now and then! He's our household mascot!'

The children spent a full happy day. Attila, Timmy and the little monkey got on famously! They gambolled on the lawn, performing all sorts of acrobatics, and ran races. Soon even Anne was laughing heartily. The Five noticed that, now Tinker had Attila to play with, he didn't feel he had to pretend to be a car or a lorry the whole time – that was a habit of his which used to be quite a nuisance!

When evening came, after a delicious supper of sausages and new green peas, Jenny's special jam tarts, and crisp apples for anyone who had any room left, the children went to bed quite early. They all felt a little tired after such an exciting day. George and Anne were to share a room on the first floor. Tinker's own bedroom was on the second floor, and Julian and Dick had been given a room next to his. The three boys fell asleep quite soon.

George and Anne stayed awake for a little while, talking, in their own bedroom. Anne, who was quite exhausted, was the first to close her eyes.

George smiled. 'Timmy, old boy,' she whispered to her dog, who was stretched out on the rug beside her bed, 'it's time we went to sleep too! I should think I'll sleep like a log until morning!'

But she was wrong!

In the middle of the night, George was suddenly woken by a strange noise. Someone seemed to be moving around outside in the garden, in a stealthy way.

'That must be Attila,' George thought at once. 'Tinker told us he was as good as a watchdog, and guarded the house at night.' But to set her mind at rest, she got out of bed and went over to the window in the dark.

At first she couldn't make anything out. Then,

straining her eyes, she thought she saw a shadowy shape moving – or maybe *two* shadowy shapes. She spotted something slipping into the bushes, and then there was an odd noise – a sort of muffled gurgling. However, just then the wind rose, rustling all the leaves of the trees in the big garden, and however hard George listened, she couldn't hear any more. She stood watching for a moment longer, and then shrugged her shoulders.

'It's only my imagination,' she told herself. 'I enjoy having adventures so much that I expect I sometimes imagine things which aren't there at all! If any burglars *had* tried getting into Big Hollow, Attila would have raised the alarm by now!'

With that thought she went back to bed, almost disappointed! The fact was, George loved mysteries and adventures – her lively, intelligent mind was quick to rise to that sort of challenge! As George's cousins knew, she was a real tomboy and a daredevil too, always on the go, and she had led the rest of the Five into all sorts of adventures. Sometimes they had solved mysteries which even baffled the police.

However, when George got up next morning, she realised she had *not* been imagining things. She and Anne came down to the dining room to find the three boys already there – and Tinker, Julian and Dick seemed to be puzzled and upset. They told the girls that Attila the cheetah had disappeared!

George scented a mystery at once! Feeling very interested, she immediately asked her cousins and Tinker exactly what they knew about it.

'Jenny's just told us that he isn't in the garden,' Tinker said. 'She called and called him to come for his breakfast, but nothing happened. And he usually comes running the moment he hears her voice. But there was no sign of him today – poor Jenny looked everywhere, but she couldn't find him! I just can't make it out!'

'Why don't we go out and search for him ourselves?' Julian suggested. 'If you ask me, Attila looks every bit as mischievous as Mischief himself! He might be hiding from us in the shrubbery – or among those trees at the end of the garden. Let's go and look!'

Professor Hayling was already at work in his study. The children wondered if he had been to bed at all! Sometimes he stayed shut up in his study for days on end, working on his beloved figures, just snatching a few hours' sleep now and then on a camp bed. When that happened, he would ask Jenny to bring him trays of food at the most peculiar times! Since he was so absorbed in his work, the children were left to do much as they liked.

They were already starting off to look for Attila, when George said, 'I think we ought to ask Jenny a few questions first.'

They found the housekeeper in the kitchen.

'Oh dear – I don't know what *I* can tell you,' she said, sighing. 'When I gave Attila his supper yesterday he was prowling round the garden, just as usual. And this morning he's simply gone – vanished without trace! There's a good stout fence all round the garden, and nowhere he could possibly have got through it. It's too high for him to have jumped over it, too. The Professor will be furious when he knows!'

'Would you mind waiting a little while before you tell him, Jenny?' asked Julian, speaking for all of them. 'We thought we'd mount our own search party!'

Jenny shook her head. 'Well, I really don't know what you can hope to find!' she sighed. 'Attila seems to have vanished into thin air!'

The children methodically searched the whole of the big garden, with the help of Timmy and Mischief, but it was no use. They found no trace of the cheetah, and they simply couldn't make out what had happened.

Then George suddenly frowned ... she was remembering the strange noises she had heard and the movements she had seen from her window last night! Her cousins and Tinker listened in silence while she told them about it.

'And if you ask me,' she finished, 'Attila's been kidnapped! Someone must have got hold of a key to the garden gate, and then slipped in secretly last night.'

'But why?' asked Anne, puzzled. 'Why would they have kidnapped a cheetah?'

'Easy!' cried Dick. 'Because they were burglars wanting to get into the house, and Attila might have raised the alarm! I expect they'll come back again tonight!'

Julian shook his head.

'I don't think so,' he said. 'You see, they could

have burgled the place last night if they'd wanted to – because after all, Attila *didn't* raise the alarm!'

'And as he didn't raise the alarm,' George added, 'he was probably drugged!'

'Or poisoned!' Dick suggested.

'Oh, don't!' said Anne, shuddering.

'Don't be silly, Dick,' said Julian, patting his sister comfortingly on the back. 'He can't have been poisoned, or we'd have found his body.'

'Unless someone wanted it for a hearth-rug,' Tinker pointed out gloomily.

'No,' said George suddenly. 'If you ask me, they *wanted* to kidnap him and that was *all* they wanted. That was why they came!'

'But why?' Anne asked again.

'If we just wait,' said George, 'I think we'll soon find out.'

When Professor Hayling had been told what had happened, he was obviously almost as upset as Tinker! But being so wrapped up in his work at the moment, he said he'd put off deciding what to do about it until next day.

'It's possible that Attila has simply run away,' he said. 'He may come back tonight, when he feels hungry. If not, I'll get in touch with the police in the morning.'

Next morning, however, there was another surprise in store for Tinker and his guests at Big Hollow House . . .

Chapter Three

A LETTER

In the morning, Jenny found a letter addressed to Professor Hayling in the letter-box by the front gate, which was where the postman always left the Professor's mail. However, this letter hadn't come by post in the usual way. There was no stamp or postmark on it – somebody had simply slipped it into the letter-box. It was a letter that would turn the whole household upside down!

As soon as Jenny set eyes on the envelope, she thought there was something funny about it. It was very poor quality paper, and rather crumpled and dirty. What was more, the address was very clumsily written – in enormous capital letters.

Jenny took the envelope to Professor Hayling, who opened it in his usual absent-minded way – but as soon as he had read the letter inside, he uttered a loud cry.

'Jenny! Tinker! What impudence – *daring* to give me orders! Threatening me – *me*!'

Hearing all the noise he was making, the

children came running in. Jenny tried in vain to calm the Professor down. He was waving his arms about in the air, in a terrible rage. Tinker asked his father what the matter was.

'The matter?' shouted the Professor, waving the letter at him. 'Attila's been kidnapped, that's the matter – and the scoundrels who did it are demanding a king's ransom for him!'

Tinker, Julian, Dick and Anne all looked at George – so she'd guessed right, as usual!

'Are they asking for a tremendous lot of money, Professor?' asked Julian.

'No, not a penny – it's worse than that! Attila's kidnappers say I must give them the formula for the amazing new fuel I've just invented for car engines! And if I don't . . .' The Professor put his head in his hands.

'*What* if you don't?' asked Tinker, feeling very much alarmed.

The Professor sighed heavily. 'If I don't,' he went on, 'those criminals will starve Attila, and once he's become a savage wild beast again they'll let him loose. Just imagine the panic a wild animal like that would spread among the villages here, children! Poor Attila would be starving, so he'd have to find food somehow – he'd begin killing farm animals. And as he belongs to me, I'd be held responsible for the damage! But the worst of it is that people would be sure to organise a hunt, and when they found Attila they'd shoot him!'

'Shoot Attila? Oh no – I don't *want* him to be shot!' protested Tinker.

'No, we can't let that happen!' Dick agreed.

'They're giving me two days to think it over and come to my decision,' Professor Hayling went on. 'Meanwhile, they say, I'll be receiving a second letter, giving me directions for delivering the ransom and getting Attila back.'

'Surely you won't agree to give them the formula?' exclaimed Julian.

'Well, children, I'm faced with a cruel choice! Either I resign myself to seeing our pet turn wild and spread terror through the countryside, until he's finally tracked down and shot, or I agree to give them the formula of my fuel, so that they can make a fortune out of it just for themselves!'

'Oh, sir!' cried poor Jenny, near tears. 'Do find some way to stop them killing Attila. It's not his fault, poor creature!'

* * *

The children did not see Tinker's father again until supper that evening. The five of them spent the rest of the day searching the garden once more, looking in vain for any clues left behind by the cheetah's kidnappers.

Timmy did all he could to help George. His keen nose took him as far as the gateway, but though the kidnappers had obviously come in and out through the gate, Timmy lost the scent as soon as he was beyond it.

'They must have given Attila a powerful tranquilliser to knock him out, and then taken him away by car,' Julian deduced.

Poor little Mischief, too, was doing all *he* could to find his friend the cheetah. But he had no luck either!

At supper, Professor Hayling told the children what he had decided.

'I've thought it all over carefully.' he said, 'and I'm not going to give them the secret of my super-fuel in exchange for Attila. I really am very sorry, Tinker, but there's nothing else I can do. You see, children, it's not my own interests at stake – I'm not holding on to my formula just so as to sell it to the highest bidder! I intend to make a gift of it to the nation, and it will benefit the whole community!'

Tinker blinked hard to keep back his tears. The other children lowered their heads, and Jenny, who had just put a dish of potatoes down on the table, dabbed at her eyes with a corner of her apron. They all knew that Professor Hayling was right, but they felt so sorry for the cheetah! Poor Attila!

After supper, Professor Hayling showed the children round his scientific laboratory.

'It was here,' he explained, 'that I developed my remarkable fuel. It's a discovery which will be useful to the whole world – no one can be allowed to keep such an invention to himself! But if I let those ruffians have it, I'm quite sure they will hurry to produce it long before the Government can, and they'll charge enormously high prices to line their own pockets!'

'I do understand,' said Julian. 'You can't save

Attila at the price of something that's so important to humanity.'

'You're right!' sighed George. 'The criminals were counting on your kind heart and your affection for the cheetah, but they didn't work things out quite right.'

'I expect they thought I'd give in for Tinker's sake,' said the Professor. 'He's so fond of Attila, and of course I don't want my son to be unhappy!'

Tinker stood up very straight. 'I have no right to ask you to sacrifice your formula, Dad!' he said proudly.

'I'm really very sorry, my boy!'

Tender-hearted Anne thought Tinker was being very noble. George was sympathetic – she knew how *she* would have felt if it had been Timmy instead of Attila! Dick, however, was so interested in Professor Hayling's amazing new fuel that he almost forgot about the cheetah.

'Have you sent the Government your formula yet, Professor Hayling?' he asked.

'Goodness me, no!' replied the scientist. 'I'm still checking the last sets of figures. Those criminals must be very well informed ... Well, you'd better leave me alone now, children. I'm going to write those people a letter refusing to give in to their blackmail!'

'Dad, do wait a little longer!' cried Tinker. He wasn't resigned to losing his beloved Attila yet. 'Why not tell the police? Perhaps *they* can find our cheetah?'

'There's not much time left, Tinker. I must

finish getting my formula worked out as soon as possible. Now that it's threatened, I shan't rest easy until I've handed it over to the authorities. And having the police around the place would waste too much time!'

The children didn't seem quite convinced!

'Don't you see?' Professor Hayling went on, rather impatiently. 'The police would come and question me, taking up my valuable time – and meanwhile I've no doubt the criminals would be thinking up some other way to gain their ends! No, we won't call in the police until my formula is safely completed! Off you go now, children.'

Anne, usually so timid, ventured to ask a question.

'Do you think Attila may be a danger to human beings if they starve him and then let him loose?'

'No, he'll only attack cows and sheep, or smaller animals. The people of Big Hollow and Little Hollow need have nothing to fear! And I suspect the criminals may not really carry out their threats. My refusal will disappoint them, and I think they'll most probably kill poor Attila and then make their getaway – empty-handed!'

Sadly, Julian, Dick, George, Anne and Tinker left the Professor's laboratory. It was still light out of doors, but the big garden seemed so empty, with no Attila prowling along the paths!

Tinker was beginning to feel angry as well as sad.

'We must *do* something!' he suddenly decided. 'I vote we try to find Attila ourselves!'

'Just what I was going to suggest!' said George.

'Since your father doesn't want to call in the police, we'll have to carry out our own inquiries. After all, we've solved mysteries before, and some of them were much more difficult!'

'You sound as if you were sure we'd be successful!' said Tinker, already feeling more hopeful.

'I'm not *sure* of anything, but why shouldn't we succeed? Specially with you to help us, Tinker! You know the countryside round here, and we must explore every inch of it.'

'Do you think the kidnappers are hiding somewhere close?'

'I'm sure they are!' replied George.

'Well, we'll get up at crack of dawn tomorrow and start our investigations without wasting any time!' said Julian.

But George shook her head. 'We can get down to work sooner than that!' she said. 'And without leaving the house and garden either!'

The others looked at her blankly.

'But we've already been all over the garden with a fine toothcomb!' Julian reminded her. 'And without any results.'

'Yes, but you're forgetting one thing,' George said. Her eyes were very bright. 'The kidnappers will be coming to *us*!'

'Coming to us?' Tinker repeated, puzzled. 'What on earth do you mean, George? Of course they won't come to us!'

'Yes, they will! Remember what your father told us – Attila's kidnappers are giving him forty-eight hours to come to a decision, but meanwhile they have to get another letter to him, giving him instructions for delivering his reply!'

'Yes, you're right! But I don't see how –'

'Hang on, I haven't finished yet! I suppose the "instructions" will be in another letter, like the one that came today. Not sent through the post – put directly into the letter-box by the gate!'

Julian gave a start of surprise. 'Of course – why didn't I think of that?' he said. 'I expect they'll deliver the second letter tonight!'

'That's what I think too.'

'George, you're a genius!' cried Tinker.

George laughed. 'Maybe not a genius, but I'm not a complete and total idiot! And I can put two and two together if I absolutely have to!'

Dick was already making plans out loud. 'We'll all keep watch in the shrubbery – all night long, if we have to!'

'But not all at once,' George said. 'We don't want to waste our manpower unnecessarily! Let's keep watch in pairs, and take turns.'

The others agreed. They decided that Julian and Anne would take the first watch, then George and Dick would take over, and then it would be Julian again, with Tinker this time.

When would the crooks turn up?

Chapter Four

A LONG NIGHT

That night seemed a very long one to the five children. Julian and Anne were the first to keep watch, as they had agreed. They crouched in a big clump of hydrangeas near the gate for what seemed like hours and hours. But nothing happened! No one came near the letter-box.

'I'll go and wake George and Dick,' whispered Julian, when it was time for them to change over. 'You wait here till they come, Anne!'

Dick and George were out of bed in a moment, ready for action. Tiptoeing out of the house so as not to wake anyone – particularly Professor Hayling or Jenny – they slipped out into the garden themselves, with Timmy at their heels.

'You stay behind the hydrangeas, Dick,' said George, 'and I'll hide behind that tree over there.'

Dick had no chance to argue, because George had already gone to her post, which was the very nearest cover she could find to the gateway!

'Now then, Timmy, old fellow,' she whispered into the dog's ear, 'I'm sure *we're* the ones who

Julian and Anne were the first to keep watch, crouched in a big clump of hydrangeas.

'Timmy, I'm sure we're the ones who will catch the criminals red — handed!'

will catch the criminals red-handed, so get ready to jump out at them!'

She had hardly finished speaking when a shadow rose silently just above the level of the letter-box. George held her breath. She could hardly see it, but she thought it was a hand – a hand in a dark glove! It must be about to drop a letter into the box!

George couldn't help letting out a yell of victory, while Timmy immediately leaped forward.

And then – then there such a racket that Dick stood rooted to the spot behind his hydrangeas, wondering what on earth was going on!

Timmy was barking as hard as ever he could – and George, who had seen her mistake too late, was trying to make him shut up. Because she had been wrong! What she had taken for a gloved hand was nothing but a big black cat, which had jumped up on top of the letter-box!

Timmy went on barking loudly, taking no notice of George. The cat, frightened but ready to fight, scratched his nose. It hissed and spat at him.

'Woof! Woof! Woof!'

'Fft! Ssss! Fft!'

Between them they made a deafening row – and what with George's yell too, everyone in Big Hollow House was roused! Professor Hayling shouted at them from his bedroom, and Jenny came to her window to see what was going on.

Feeling very disappointed, George called back to say that Timmy had got on the scent of a cat and set off to chase it. Luckily, Professor Hayling and Jenny were so sleepy that they didn't think of asking why George and Timmy were out in the garden in the first place!

Dick and George settled down to keep watch again.

'What an ass I am!' George told herself. 'I may have spoiled everything! If the kidnappers *were* somewhere near, they've probably taken fright and gone off again.'

When Julian and Tinker came to take over for the last watch, there was still no message in the letter-box. The two boys kept watch until morning, but nothing happened. They went back to bed just as the rest of the house was coming to life.

'It's all my fault,' said George gloomily, when Tinker and the four cousins were having a late breakfast of eggs and bacon in the dining room. 'If only I hadn't been so stupid, I'm sure we'd have caught the kidnappers!'

But it turned out that George needn't have blamed herself, because about ten in the morning, when Jenny went to fetch that morning's post from the letter-box she found the second message from Attila's kidnappers! This time it had not been put straight into the box outside the house after all – it had been sent by post the day before, and the postmark showed that it had been posted in Big Hollow village. The address was written in big capital letters again.

Feeling quite weak at the knees, Jenny hurried to take the letter to Professor Hayling. The children met her going along the passage, and saw the envelope in her hand.

'More news from the kidnappers?' asked Tinker, pointing to the letter.

'Oh, blow!' said Dick. 'So we spent all last night keeping watch, and it was never any use!' Then he bit his lip. Jenny looked suspiciously at the children.

'Now, you're not to get mixed up in this, you know, children! It's your father's business, Tinker! Let me by, please.'

But George and her cousins and Tinker certainly didn't intend to give up their inquiries – quite the opposite! They meant to carry on, making full use of any clues given in this new message. And so they all went off to find Professor Hayling in his laboratory.

'Dad,' said Tinker boldly, 'we know the kidnappers have sent you their instructions! How exactly do they want you to get in touch with them?'

The Professor, who was already deep in his figures again, pointed absent-mindedly to the letter, which was lying on a table.

'Oh, read it for yourself, my boy, and leave me in peace. You know what my reply will be, since I'm not going to let them have my formula! I shall write to say no, and Jenny will deliver my answer.'

Tinker picked up the letter. Like the envelope

and the first letter, it was printed in capital letters. His friends and Timmy followed him out of the laboratory.

The children went and sat in the shade of some bushes by the stream which flowed through the field behind the house. They read the letter, weighing up every word it said very carefully – even Mischief seemed to be puzzling it out!

'Well,' said George, after reading it, 'that seems clear enough! This evening, Jenny's to go to Bluebell Wood outside Big Hollow village alone, taking Professor Hayling's reply.'

'Yes,' said Dick. 'The kidnappers want her to go to the clearing in the wood – isn't that the place we explored last year?'

'And once she gets there,' said Julian, 'Jenny will find – now let's see, what did they say?'

He picked up the letter again and looked at it. 'There's an oak tree stump there, and she'll find a wicker cage on the stump – she's to put Professor Hayling's reply into the cage. If the envelope contains the formula, they say Attila will be returned during the next forty-eight hours.'

Anne looked over her brother's shoulder. 'And after leaving the reply she's to walk away from the clearing without even turning her head to look back,' she said. 'My word – if I was Jenny I'd never *dare* go there all on my own! But that's what the criminals say she must do!'

'They won't harm Jenny,' Tinker reassured her. 'But since they *won't* find the formula in the envelope, there'll be reprisals!'

'Reprisals?' asked Anne. 'What's that?'

'It means they'll take their revenge,' Julian told her. 'In other words – it's bad luck for poor Attila!'

Tinker and Anne sighed, looking very downcast. But George was already drawing up a plan of attack.

'We must act! Whatever happens, we must catch those crooks!' she said. 'Now, this is what I suggest! This evening, *we* go to the clearing in Bluebell Wood, before Jenny gets there. We'll hide near the wicker cage and wait. When the kidnappers come to collect your father's reply, Tinker, we'll follow them – and they'll lead us to the place where they're keeping your cheetah!'

'Oh, I see!' cried Tinker. 'And then we'll be able to rescue Attila and get the crooks arrested!'

'Why don't we go to the police *now*?' suggested Anne.

'Oh, Anne, don't be silly!' said Dick. 'If the police stepped in at this point, the kidnappers would be so angry they certainly wouldn't hesitate to kill Attila straight away!'

'Yes,' Julian agreed. 'All things considered, George, I think yours is a good plan. We'll creep through the wood without making a sound, and follow the criminals to their hideout.'

'And if one of them comes on his own, we can all jump out and overpower him! We could use *him* as a hostage!'

'Don't let's get carried away,' Julian advised, sensible as ever. 'We'll make up our minds what to do when we see what happens. Meanwhile, I think we all ought to have a rest and try to get some sleep this afternoon! We were up half of last night, and we'll need to get our strength back for this evening's expedition!'

George grinned. 'All right!' she said. 'Then we'll all be fighting fit for Operation Attila!'

Chapter Five

IN BLUEBELL WOOD

George, her cousins and Tinker set off at dusk. Timmy was with them, but they had decided it would be more sensible to leave Mischief at home.

They went along the lanes in silence. Soon they reached the wood, and they stopped when they came to the edge of the clearing.

'Those bushes look like a good place to hide,' whispered George. 'From there, we'll have a good view of Jenny when she comes.'

'Oh!' exclaimed Anne. 'Look – on that tree stump over there!'

'Yes!' said Dick. 'A wicker cage, just as they said! It looks very lightweight, and they've made sure it's in a prominent place.

'Ssh!' Julian hissed. 'I can hear footsteps. There's someone coming along the path – yes, it's Jenny!'

Sure enough, Jenny it was! She had no idea there were six pairs of eyes watching her movements. She had just emerged from the wood, and she was walking fast. You could tell she was in a hurry to get her dangerous mission over and done with. Was she afraid? Well, she was being very brave, and if she *was* frightened she didn't let it show! Anne was full of admiration for her.

Once in the clearing, Jenny stopped for a moment, and slowly looked round her. Then, catching sight of the tree stump, she went up to the cage and slipped Professor Hayling's reply into this unusual letter-box! After that, she turned round and went away, walking even faster than before.

When the sound of her footsteps had died away in the distance, George whispered, 'Well, *that's* done! Now for the most exciting part of our expedition. It's all up to us now!'

Julian, Dick, Anne, George and Tinker kept absolutely still, though they could feel their hearts beating very fast. The moment when they would be face to face with Attila's kidnappers was very close!

George's hand tightened on Timmy's collar. The intelligent dog knew what was expected of him, and he kept still too – he didn't move any more than the tree stump on which the wicker cage was resting!

Anne, the most timid of the children, found it hard to stay calm.

'Oh, I do hope things will turn out all right!' she said to herself. 'What will become of us if the kidnappers find us here?'

Like her brothers and cousin, she really

Jenny slipped Professor Hayling's reply into the unusual letter-box!

The dog took the handle in his mouth—and turned and trotted away with the cage!

enjoyed adventures. And like them, she was never short of courage when real danger came – it was waiting for it to come that she didn't like!

Suddenly Dick moved slightly. 'Someone's coming!' he whispered.

Timmy pricked up his ears. Yes, something *was* moving in the wood – the children strained their eyes and craned their necks to see! There was a quivering among the leaves. And suddenly a slender shape came out into the clearing – but it was only a deer! A pretty little doe.

Anne let out a sigh of relief. The others sighed too, but with impatience. They felt let down. They wished the kidnappers wouldn't keep them waiting.

They all settled down to keep watch again. Julian looked at his watch – its luminous hands said the time was quarter past ten. Suddenly, he stiffened. He had just heard another sound ...

George, Tinker, Dick and Anne had heard it too. They were all holding their breath, and Timmy followed suit. This time they *couldn't* be wrong! There really was someone creeping stealthily through the undergrowth, making dry twigs crack underfoot and setting up faint echoes in the darkness.

'Whoever it is creeping along like that is very light on his feet,' thought George, intrigued. 'It can't be a man coming, or even a woman. It's more likely a child!'

She didn't tell the others what she was thinking, because she was afraid even a whisper might give them away. She just strained her eyes

42

even harder, if possible, staring at the spot where the noise was coming from.

The moon had risen fully now, and was casting its mysterious light on the scene. George's eyes were fixed on a point at the opposite side of the clearing, quite low down among the bushes.

She was expecting to see them part at any moment, to let the figure of a child through.

However, the figure that did emerge from the bushes wasn't what George had expected! It wasn't a man or a woman – but it wasn't a child either. It was a dog – a big, black cocker spaniel!

Dick saw the dog at the same time as his cousin. 'Oh no!' he groaned. 'Another false alarm! First the deer, now this wretched dog!'

The others were disappointed, too. 'Yes, another false alarm,' Julian, Anne and Tinker agreed.

But George said nothing. She was interested in the dog who had come out of the wood. *She* didn't think this was a false alarm!

Sure enough, the dog was behaving oddly. He had stopped, one forepaw in the air, his nose pointing to the sky as if he were sniffing the wind.

Timmy was getting restless, ready to leap out at the strange dog if his young mistress gave the word. But George tapped him lightly on the nose, to let him know he mustn't move a muscle or make any noise, and the obedient dog kept perfectly still.

Meanwhile, the children were still watching the newcomer. Suddenly the spaniel seemed to make up his mind. He bounded forward, making

43

straight for the cage. It had a round wicker handle on top. Without a moment's hesitation, the dog jumped up on the tree stump, took the handle in his mouth – and turned and trotted away with the cage!

The astonished watchers had not been expecting anything like this! No one moved for several seconds. Julian, who was usually so calm, couldn't help giving an exclamation of annoyance.

'Oh, blow it all – that dog's stealing the kidnappers' letter-box!'

'No – I think he belongs to them, and he's specially trained to act as their messenger!' said Tinker, in despair. 'And we'll never be able to catch up with him, so we've lost the trail again!'

George shook herself, and jumped up. For a moment she had almost given way to despair herself. But she wasn't someone who would ever admit herself beaten, as she proved once again.

'We're not finished yet!' she cried. 'Not by a very long chalk! Those wicked kidnappers have a dog, but so have we. Come on, Tim, old boy! It's time for you to show what you can do! You're more intelligent than any old cocker spaniel, aren't you?'

Tinker looked very surprised. 'But how can Timmy help us?' he asked.

Instead of replying, George knelt down beside Timmy. Putting her arms round his neck, she told him, 'Follow that dog, Timmy! Catch up with him – but no fighting, old boy, do you understand? Go on, then! Seek him! Find out where he's going and then come back here. I'll be waiting. Do you understand, Timmy? Off you go, then – quick!'

'Woof!' said Timmy.

And with one bound, he set off after the black cocker spaniel. The children watched him disappear among the bushes.

Dick looked doubtfully at his cousin.

'Well, I know old Timmy *is* a very intelligent dog,' he said, shaking his head, 'but all the same – are you sure he understood all that?'

'Positive!'

Dick shook his head again. 'Just for once, I think you're putting too much faith in Timmy!'

'If you ask me,' said Tinker, 'he'll follow that dog all right, and catch up with him – then there'll be a fight, and that's all.'

'Oh no, you're wrong!' George assured them, looking quite offended. 'Timmy understood perfectly well, and he knows he musn't fight the other dog. I've trained him to know all my tones of voice. *And* I've trained him to chase the cats who come trespassing in our garden at home in Kirrin Cottage, but not to hurt them. That's what he'll do with the dog we saw! All we have to do is wait for him to come back, and then I'll get him to lead us to wherever the cocker spaniel went – and we'll know where the kidnappers are hiding! Then we'll decided what to do next, just as Julian suggested!'

Julian, Dick, Anne and Tinker looked at George with mingled admiration and respect. She really *had* thought of everything! Like a good general, she could show initiative and act fast. Thanks to her, their expedition might yet turn out successful – if Timmy really did as she'd told him!

'You're really quite clever, for a girl!' Dick told her.

George looked cross. She didn't like people reminding her she was a girl – she'd so much rather have been a boy! However, she realised that Dick *meant* to pay her a compliment!

'All we have to do now is wait,' she said.

'Wait how long?' asked Anne.

Julian smiled. 'That depends how far the cocker spaniel has to go!' he told his little sister. 'But I shouldn't think it can be *very* far. That wicker cage may be light to carry, but it's bound to be a nuisance to the dog as he runs along, and his jaws will get tired. However well-trained he may be, he'll feel like putting down what he's carrying some time. And then his attention might wander and he'd forget to pick it up again. I don't think the kidnappers would have wanted to take a risk like that and make him go a very long way, so I'm pretty sure they can't be far off.'

'I hope not!' sighed George. 'Well, we'll have to be patient.'

They all sat round in a circle on the moss in the clearing. They weren't afraid of being seen now. To make the time pass, they discussed the whole situation as they waited.

However, more and more time went by, and still Timmy didn't come back. At last Anne told the others something that was worrying her.

46

'Suppose Timmy doesn't come back at all?'

George withered her cousin with a glance.

'Timmy – not come back? Don't be silly, Anne! He'd never disobey me, you know that quite well!'

'That – that's not exactly what I meant!' stammered poor Anne. 'If the kidnappers see him they may do something to hurt him. And I'd hate it if anything happened to Timmy!'

The poor little girl had tears in her eyes at the mere thought of it. George shrugged her shoulders, and said in a rough voice which didn't quite hide her own feelings, 'You're not going to weep buckets all over us before anything *does* happen, are you? Anyway, why should anything happen to Tim? He's very good at getting out of a fix – he's not one of the Five for nothing!'

She was interrupted by the sound of twigs breaking, followed by a brief bark.

'Woof!'

'Timmy! Here's Timmy!' And George, radiant, rushed to meet her dog as he came bounding up.

'Well done, Tim! You did it, didn't you? Now, one more effort, old boy! Lead us to that dog! Come on, back on the trail – and we'll follow you!'

Chapter Six

A DEAD END!

A moment later, the five children were following Timmy right into the wood. They felt a surge of hope! If Tim *did* lead them to the place where Attila's kidnappers were hiding, perhaps they'd be able to set the big cat free that very night.

Tinker walked ahead of his friends, taking no notice of the brambles which scratched him as he went along. He was ready for anything that would get his beloved cheetah back! He'd face any kind of danger!

Of course, Timmy and the cocker spaniel had covered the distance much faster than the children could – they had four paws, while the children only had their two legs each! In the dark, Anne often stumbled over treacherous, unseen tree roots, and her brothers had to catch her to stop her falling.

George, who was feeling impatient, kept muttering under her breath.

'Oh, hurry up, do! Don't dawdle! Take longer

strides, can't you, Anne? You're making us lose precious time!'

'Stop bullying her!' Julian told George. 'You're forgetting she's the smallest of us.'

George had a kind heart, and she slowed down. But Timmy seemed to be in as much of a hurry as she was – he ran ahead, going so fast that he seemed to be in danger of leaving the rest of them behind any moment. George had to call him back. At last the children came out of the wood.

'Now for it!' said Dick.

'Which way do we go now, Tim?' George asked.

The children were on top of a small hill which went down a gentle slope towards the sea. The sea itself was like a silvery lake in the moonlight. Behind them was the wood, with the village of Big Hollow beyond it. Ahead of them there was only the sea and the sky. Without hesitating, Timmy set off along a path down to the shore. Julian looked round him and whistled.

'That's funny,' he murmured. 'Timmy's taking us down to the beach. But there's no house or hut anywhere there – and the beach itself is flat as a pancake! I hope your dog hasn't made a mistake, George.'

'Just trust him,' George said. 'Though I must say, *I* think it's funny too. I don't see *any* place where the kidnappers could be hiding!'

But this was no time for talking. The five friends set off again, following Timmy. Once he was down on the fine sand of the beach, the dog

The sea was like a silvery lake in the moonlight.

stopped for a moment, and then, nose to the ground, started going round and round on the spot in little circles, sniffing noisily the whole time.

'Are you on the scent of something, old boy?' George asked.

Realising that they were alone on the beach, Julian took a torch out of his pocket. He switched it on and directed the beam at the sand. Dick, Tinker, George and Anne uttered an exclamation!

Now they could see what Timmy was sniffing at – something the moonlight had been too faint to show them at first.

'Footsteps!' cried Anne.

'And the tracks of another dog's paws, as well as Timmy's,' said George.

'There were two men here!' added Tinker, who had crouched down to take a closer look. 'These tracks were made by two different sizes of shoes – or more likely gumboots, I should think.'

'And all the tracks are going towards the sea,' Dick pointed out gloomily. 'They stop at the water's edge. That speaks for itself!'

'I'm afraid it does!' sighed Julian. 'We don't need second sight to be able to tell what happened here – not so very long ago, either!'

'You're right, Ju!' said George, dismayed. 'The kidnappers came by boat, sent the cocker spaniel off to the clearing, and when he came back with the wicker cage containing the message, they simply got back into their boat with him and went away by sea!'

Now what? Yes, that was the question! If the

kidnappers had left by sea, where exactly had they been going? The children were no nearer solving that problem than before.

Dick exclaimed in annoyance. 'They could be staying in any of the villages near the coast!' he said.

Julian switched his torch off. 'Or they may be sheltering in a cave – there are lots of caves near here,' he said. 'That would be even more convenient for them, because of hiding the cheetah!'

'Well, we can't just stand around here,' said George. 'Can we, Tinker?'

Tinker himself had no intention of turning back and going home to bed – anyway, he knew he'd never be able to sleep. Were they going to own themselves beaten when they'd been so close to getting on Attila's trail? Never!

So he agreed with George. 'Yes, we must do something!' he cried. 'The only thing is, though – what?'

But George was never short of ideas.

'We must work it all out logically,' she told the others, who had gathered round her. 'If those men came by boat, it could have been to make sure they left no trail behind them – *and* to hide the fact that they're staying quite close!'

'Hm – yes, that's possible,' Julian said.

'And it's possible, too,' George went on, 'that they may have gone to earth somewhere near. They haven't had time to get very far by boat. The tide's coming in now, and it will soon have wiped any prints they may have left if we don't hurry. So we must act at once!'

'What are you getting at?' asked Dick.

'Well, I know there are two little bays just down the coast from here. They might be worth exploring! If we're in luck, we may yet find out where your cheetah is tonight, Tinker.'

'Oh, I know those bays too,' cried the boy. 'In fact, I can show you a short cut to them! Don't forget that I live near here!'

'Good, Tinker – that'll save us going the long way round by road.'

But Julian felt that these hasty investigations weren't likely to get them anywhere. Indeed, he feared they might be running into trouble. 'We could be walking straight into the lion's den,' he warned the others.

'Oh, come on, Ju!' cried George. 'Nothing venture, nothing win! We can't just go back to Big Hollow empty-handed! And there are five of us, after all – seven if you count Timmy, because he's as good as two in a tight place. *And* we have right on our side! And Attila will be on our side too if we do find him, and I bet *he's* as good as even two of Timmy in a fight, and then –'

'And then, and then, and then – oh, that'll do! Stop talking so much!' Dick interrupted. 'Come on, let's start by exploring the nearest of the two bays. You show us the way, Tinker. Lead on and we'll follow!'

Julian and Anne – who really would have liked to go home now – realised that they were in a minority, so they gave in. But Julian, as the eldest and most responsible, was worried. He wasn't as impetuous as his cousin, and he was afraid that George's rashness might be letting them in for trouble.

After they had taken Tinker's short cut across a promontory, walking over big round pebbles polished by the sea, which crunched underfoot, the children came down on the beach of the first bay.

'Be careful!' Julian warned everyone. 'I'll go scouting ahead, with Dick. The rest of you stay here, and don't move.'

But George insisted on going with the scouting party too, and Timmy, of course, wouldn't be parted from her. So Tinker and Anne watched the other four set off down to the open, sandy part of the beach.

This time Julian didn't dare switch his torch on. If the kidnappers had made their headquarters in one of the caves which riddled the cliff face, the light might put them on their guard.

'This is where Timmy will really come in useful!' whispered George. 'Go on – seek! Good dog! Seek, Timmy!'

But though Timmy sniffed about, nose to the ground, he didn't find anything. The kidnappers could not have been this way. Realising this, Julian took the risk of shining his torch quickly on the sand. There were no tracks in it at all! Timmy's nose wasn't letting him down – it was just that no one had been here since the last high tide.

54

Disappointed, the four of them went back to Tinker and Anne.

'Let's have one last try and explore the second bay,' said George. However, she wasn't very hopeful now, and nor were the others. They set off in silence, with Tinker in the lead.

No – they didn't find any tracks on the beach in the second bay either. And the village of Little Hollow came down to the sea in the next bay along the coast – there would be no hope of identifying footprints on a beach where so many went bathing in summer. The trail had petered out!

It was a sad little procession that set off back to Big Hollow village, which was farther inland than Little Hollow. Poor Anne didn't even dare to say how tired she was, and Tinker, realising that his beloved Attila was really lost, had a hard time keeping back his tears. Oh, if only he could get his hands on those kidnappers!

The children slipped into the house very quietly and went up to their rooms. Luckily Professor Hayling and Jenny had no idea at all that they had been out – or the children would have felt worse than ever about coming home empty-handed.

As for George, she was still feeling absolutely furious. She had had such great hopes of the success of their expedition, and they had set off so boldly! But luck just hadn't been on her side, as she had to admit.

Well, who knew? Tomorrow was another day – and maybe luck *would* be with her then!

Chapter Seven

A LETTER FOR TINKER

Next day the sun shone down from a cloudless sky. A warm breeze gently swayed the treetops in the garden. It was a really wonderful summer's day – or it would have been, but for the gloomy faces of the young people at Big Hollow House!

The children got up that morning feeling very downcast. Poor Tinker's eyes were red-rimmed. He had been crying, alone in his room – Julian and Dick didn't like to look at him. Anne was near tears herself, and George was feeling so angry that she kept clenching her fists inside her pockets.

As for Jenny, she was sniffling as she gave the children their breakfast. The poor housekeeper was sighing so heavily that in any other circumstance it would have been quite funny!

In all this gloom, only Professor Hayling seemed much the same as usual. That was because he had put Attila and the kidnappers out of his mind once and for all, and was concentrating on his formula. It would very soon be ready now – and just think of all it would lead to! The Professor was thrilled by the idea.

'It's not that Dad's heartless,' Tinker explained to his friends, when Professor Hayling had gone back to his laboratory after breakfast. 'But he's so wrapped up in his work that he forgets about everything else.'

Jenny's unhappiness was making her rather short-tempered. 'If you've quite finished eating,' she told the children crossly, 'for goodness' sake don't stay shut up indoors! It's beautiful weather. Go and play outside – or take your bicycles and go for a ride in the country.'

However, Tinker and his friends didn't feel like going for a bicycle ride, though they did go out into the garden so as not to be in Jenny's way. But once outside, there wasn't any particular game that the children wanted to play. They all felt too sad.

'I don't feel like doing *anything*, now that Attila's gone,' said Tinker.

'If only we had one little clue!' said George. 'Then we could go on trying to find your cheetah. But as it is –'

A sudden exclamation from Dick interrupted her.

As they talked, the children, together with Timmy and Mischief, had reached the garden gate. It was before the time when the postman usually came, but all the same, Dick had spotted a white envelope inside the letter-box. 'A letter!' he said. 'Look – inside the box there!'

Like Dick, the others saw something white in the letter-box too.

'What can it be?' asked Anne, surprised and alarmed.

But of course the other children had guessed at once!

Tinker ran to open the box, and took out an envelope with the address printed in big capitals. No one was a bit surprised. They all knew that this must be another letter sent by Attila's kidnappers – or rather, *brought* by Attila's kidnappers, since it hadn't come in the post!

George went first red and then white with anger. Dick made such a sudden, violent movement that he frightened Mischief, who ran to bury his face in Tinker's neck for safety.

'Oh *no*!' cried Dick. 'If only we'd been keeping watch in the garden *last* night, instead of the night before, we'd have caught them in the act.'

But Julian shook his head. 'You can't know that,' he said. 'They may have left the letter here yesterday evening, while we were still out exploring the two bays.'

'I don't think so,' said Tinker. 'They'll have needed more time than that. For a start, they had to find out what Dad's answer was. Then they must have held a council of war, and after that they'll have had to write another letter – *and* bring it here! Of course, if we'd thought of keeping watch from the moment we got back . . .'

George kicked the gravel of the path.

'Oh, don't waste any more time talking!' she said impatiently. 'All that matters now is finding out what's in the envelope. Hurry up and take it to your father, Tinker!'

Tinker automatically glanced at the address again before he set off with the envelope. Suddenly, his eyes nearly popped out of his head.

'Hallo!' he cried. 'Why, this letter isn't for my father at all – it's addressed to *me*!'

'You?' asked the four cousins in chorus.

'That's right. Look – it says "Master T. Hayling". That's me!'

'Quick, open it!' Anne begged him.

But Tinker had already torn the envelope open. He took out a sheet of paper, and unfolded it with a hand that trembled slightly. George was urging him to hurry.

'Come on, slow-coach! Read it out loud!'

Tinker obeyed, but as his voice was shaking even more than his hands, George, unable to bear the suspense any longer, snatched the piece of paper from his fingers. 'Do you mind?' she asked. 'Sorry, Tinker, but there's no time to be lost! Listen, everyone! I'll read it out loud.'

The others all gathered round George. Timmy too was looking at his young mistress as if *he* were listening attentively to what she was saying. Mischief was listening as well. Perhaps he had a vague idea that they were talking about his friend Attila.

' "Your father has refused to give us the ransom we want in exchange for your pet cheetah," ' George read aloud. ' "We know that you are very

59

fond of the animal, so now we are making *you* an offer." '

George stopped to look at the others, who were hanging on every word, especially Tinker. His eyes and mouth were both wide open!

Feeling very excited herself, George cleared her throat, and went on reading aloud in a steady voice.

' "If you want to see your pet again, you must steal the formula for the super-fuel your father has invented and let us have it. You are sure to be able to get into his laboratory. If you don't do as we say, you can expect trouble for yourself and your friends, and the cheetah will die. So bring the formula to the clearing in Bluebell Wood yourself, at ten in the evening next Thursday. And one last warning – come alone, and don't breathe a word about this to anyone!" '

Of course, the letter wasn't signed. 'It's the same time and place as yesterday,' said Dick.

'But I can't go behind my father's back!' cried Tinker, very upset.

'Of course you can't!' said George briskly. 'Don't worry, we'll find some way to get round that. Meanwhile, we have four days ahead of us!'

Julian looked at his cousin with genuine admiration, and not for the first time either! George might be a couple of years younger than he was, but she could reason things out amazingly fast. Standing legs akimbo, she was issuing orders like a captain commanding her troops!

'Now, here's what we'll do!' she began.

The others never for a moment thought of objecting. George was a natural leader, and they were quite happy to do as she said.

'We have four days' grace,' she went on. 'We must use those four days to make inquiries in all the nearby villages.'

'Oh, yes!' cried Tinker, whose hopes had revived now that he realised his friend Attila was still alive, and would have a few days' reprieve. 'You're right, George. Let's start straight away!'

'We'll tackle Big Hollow village itself first, and then go on to Little Hollow,' George decided. 'We'll explore any suspicious places in or around those two villages. Then we'll go up the coast to Demon's Rocks village. Timmy's nose will be a help – let's take him to have a good sniff round the shed where Attila used to sleep!'

Chapter Eight

A THIEF IS CAUGHT!

Less than ten minutes later, the Five and Tinker were on their way. They did take Mischief this time, thinking he might be useful. And so he was – any time the children came to a deserted old farm building which might have been used to hide the cheetah, if they couldn't get into it themselves they sent Mischief! He could jump in anywhere – over walls and rooftops, through tiny little windows. But it was no use. He didn't find Attila.

Now and then Timmy was given a piece of cloth which Attila had slept on to sniff, and he would set off with new enthusiasm! But he still hadn't found any trace of a scent. Tinker insisted on stopping almost everywhere.

'We're wasting time,' George said crossly. 'Once we're sure Timmy isn't going to pick up a scent somewhere, we might as well go on!'

'Wait a moment, do. He *could* be wrong.'

'Timmy *wrong*?' exclaimed George, firing up at once. 'He's never been wrong in all his life! He has a nose like a bloodhound's!'

The children had been all over Big Hollow by now, and most of Little Hollow too. Anne sighed. She was feeling discouraged.

'Aren't we ever going to find anything?'

'Of course we are!' said George. 'Come on!'

So they went on ... and suddenly, Timmy stopped in front of the doorway of what looked like an old barn. The lower part of the door was rotten. The dog sniffed around it for a long time, and then began to growl. His hair stood on end.

'Hallo, that's interesting!' said Dick, lowering his voice. 'Looks as though old Timmy's found something.'

The barn was next to a small farm. The children could see squawking chickens in the farmyard, scurrying around a woman who was throwing them some grain. And above the noise the chickens were making, they heard a man's voice. The man sounded cross.

'Nearly got the scoundrel who's been stealing our fowls this time, but he gave me the slip again. Where in the world did he go, I wonder?'

'We need a dog, Bob,' said the farmer's wife. 'Since old Spot died, our hen-house has been raided far too often for my liking!'

'Hear that?' Tinker whispered to his friends. 'Someone's been stealing this farmer's chickens. It could be the kidnappers – to feed Attila!'

'But they were going to starve him – they wouldn't do that by giving him chickens to eat!' Julian sensibly pointed out. 'George, I wonder what kind of a scent Timmy's picked up there!'

George put her hand over Timmy's nose to stop him barking. Then she whispered in his ear, 'Seek! Seek, boy!'

And Timmy started scratching the ground in front of the doorway as hard as he could.

'Oh, do be careful!' cried Anne, terrified. 'The kidnappers may be inside there!'

'Or more likely Attila!' said Tinker.

'Or even more likely, none of them!' said George impatiently. 'Don't be silly – this barn isn't the kind of place for the kidnappers' hideout, *or* a prison for Attila. It's not nearly private enough. I'd really love to get in there and see if we could pick up any clues about them – something to show they'd been here!'

'It looks completely deserted,' said Dick. 'It shouldn't be difficult to force our way in.'

'No, don't!' cried Julian. 'We have no right to –'

But Dick, after glancing round to make sure there was no one coming down the road, had already put his shoulder to the door and was pushing with all his might. The effect was sudden and violent – the two halves of the door swung open, catapulting Dick into the barn on top of a whole heap of gardening tools, all rather rusty. It was a miracle he didn't hurt himself as he fell!

Of course, he made such a tremendous racket, tumbling in on all those metal tools, that it could have been heard right at the other end of the village.

'Dick, are you hurt?' cried Anne.

'No, I'm all right, but –'

Timmy began to growl.

'Keep away from me, will you?' cried the chicken thief.

Furious barking from Timmy cut him short. The dog had bounded towards one corner of the barn, and now, with his teeth bared and his coat bristling, he was holding someone at bay. Running across to seize her dog, George saw what looked like a very hairy tramp. The man was shaking with terror, and clumsily trying to hide something behind his back – two chickens! Obviously he had wrung their necks only a few minutes before! The children guessed what had happened at once.

'Hallo,' said Julian. 'I bet you anything this is the man who's been stealing the farmer's chickens!'

'Don't move!' George told the man. 'If you do, my dog will go for your throat!'

'Keep him away from me, will you?' cried the chicken thief, plainly terrified.

At that moment, they heard heavy footsteps outside the barn. Hearing the noise, the farmer and one of his men had come hurrying along to find out what had happened.

'What's all this?' the farmer began. Then he saw the chickens! 'My fowls! So *that's* where he went! Caught this thief in the act, did you, children? Well done! I was wondering where he could be hiding after he gave me the slip just now, but I never thought of looking so close to home!'

'It was my dog who picked up his scent!' explained George proudly. 'You can hand him over to the police now. Here, Timmy – good boy! Well done!'

The farmer smiled at George, while the other

man took hold of the thief by the collar. The tramp looked very crestfallen now!

And well done, yourself, my boy!' the farmer told George, thinking she *was* a boy! 'But for you, I dare say I'd have lost a good many more of my fowls. Can't spend my whole time guarding the hen-house! So thank you, young man!' And he gave George a hearty slap on the back. She stood up to it bravely, like the real boy she'd have liked to be!

Tinker seized his opportunity to ask the farmer some questions. He went straight to the point.

'Sir, we're looking for a cheetah,' he said. 'Have you by any chance seen one around here?'

The farmer looked at him in surprise, and then burst out laughing.

'Looking for a cheetah? Oh, you mean you're looking for the zoo! You might be able to see a cheetah there! The new zoo is a little way outside Little Hollow Village.'

Dick eagerly interrupted. 'Oh yes, I'd forgotten the zoo!'

'Isn't that what you wanted? It was started up only this summer – I don't think they've had very many visitors so far.'

When the farmer and his labourer had gone off, taking the chicken thief away with them, the children stood in the doorway of the deserted barn, wondering what to do next.

'Where shall we go now?' asked Anne, rather bewildered by what had just happened.

'I vote we go to the zoo!' said Dick.

'The zoo?' asked Julian.

'Why not?' said Dick. 'Anyone who stole Attila so easily must know how to handle wild beasts. Maybe the kidnappers are the people who own this zoo. Or they could be keepers who work there.'

'Yes,' said George. 'And if so, what could be easier than for them to keep the cheetah in one of the zoo's cages? Under the very noses of the visitors! It's the last place anyone would think of looking for him. That's a smashing idea, Dick – let's go and look at the animals in the zoo!'

But Julian stopped the others as they were about to hurry off.

'Half a mo!' he said. 'If we go there during opening hours, and if the kidnappers really *do* work at the zoo, they'll recognise Tinker and suspect something. They seem to be very well informed. They must know Tinker by sight!'

'You're right,' said George, disappointed. 'Too bad! Well, we'll go after the zoo closes tonight. Luckily the weather's very warm at the moment, in fact almost tropical, so I don't suppose they shut the animals up indoors for the night. We should be able to find Attila's cage easily – if he's really there, of course!'

And that night, feeling hopeful once more, the children set off for Little Hollow again. The afternoon's investigations had produced no results. But perhaps they'd do better at the zoo!

Chapter Nine

A VISIT TO THE ZOO

They soon reached the zoo. It was in the middle of a big, flat field, and it had a wooden fence all round it. Tinker soon found a gap in the fence – no doubt made by someone who wanted to get in without paying!

They agreed to leave Anne outside to keep watch, with Timmy to protect her. Julian, Dick, George and Tinker made their way in.

One by one, the four children went through the gap in the fence. Once they were the other side, they stopped to look round. The moon lit up the scene, shining down from a slightly luminous sky, as it had done the night before.

'There's something over there,' Tinker whispered. 'On my right!'

But it was only an enclosure with two ostriches in it. They were fast asleep and didn't move. George, who could see in the dark almost as well as a cat, pointed to a group of square shapes on the right.

'Over there!' she whispered. 'Those must be the animal cages!'

The four of them started cautiously advancing, afraid of making a noise and rousing someone.

There were two lionesses and a lion asleep inside the first cage. They didn't move a whisker. The children came to the second cage, and Tinker couldn't help giving a squeal of joy. There was a cheetah inside it!

'Attila!' he whispered huskily. 'Attila!'

The cheetah slowly got to its feet and went up to the bars of the cage, looking interested in Tinker, but not in the least as if it knew him. Which wasn't surprising – because it wasn't Attila at all, as Tinker could see when he had a closer look at the animal.

'You're sure?' asked Dick, seeing how disappointed his friend was.

'Yes, I'm afraid so! Attila has a white patch on this side of his nose. Oh, bother! We've drawn a blank yet again!'

However, the four friends stuck to their plan of going all round the zoo, looking for another cheetah. Not surprisingly, that was just a waste of time. They turned back sadly. But Mischief didn't seem to want to go with them . . .

The little monkey had been acting in a restless, excited way for some time, but Tinker had been so absorbed in searching the zoo that he hadn't paid enough attention to his pet. Finally, Mischief left his perch on Tinker's shoulder with a tremendous leap, and uttering happy little cries he jumped up

71

and clung to the bars of a cage which contained other monkeys – one of them the same sort of monkey as Mischief himself, though a bit larger.

'Mischief!' called Tinker. 'Come here, will you?'

But Mischief wasn't listening. Nose pressed to the bars, he was reaching his skinny arms into the cage, and seemed to be calling to the monkey who looked most like him.

The other monkey, interested, came closer. Soon the two animals were having quite a conversation!

'We'd better go,' Dick said. 'There's no point in hanging about any longer. Catch your monkey, Tinker!'

That was easier said than done – because by stretching, and making himself very thin, Mischief had just managed to squeeze in between the bars of the cage. And in the very nick of time, from *his* point of view! Now he was swinging from a branch beside the monkey who might almost have been his twin. He seemed to be deliriously excited!

At his wits' end, Tinker tried to make Mischief come back, whispering in an undertone.

'Mischief, come *here*! Come here this minute!'

But the little monkey was far too happy amongst other monkeys to pay any attention! He took no notice at all. Shrill cries were coming from the cage, as all the monkeys greeted the newcomer in their own ways, with squeals of pleasure, anger or indignation. Soon they were making a dreadful racket. Julian looked round in alarm.

'For goodness' sake, Tinker! We'd better leave

Mischief where he is and come back to fetch him tomorrow. If we stay here –'

But his advice came too late.

The noise the monkeys were making had roused two of the zoo keepers. And now they both came on the scene, shining torches at the cages. One of them was carrying a shotgun.

'Hallo, it's only a bunch of kids!' said one keeper, catching the children in the beam of his torch. 'Four kids, come along to – to do what, eh?'

'To try and pinch one of our monkeys, by the looks of it!' said the second keeper, chuckling.

George was very indignant.

'We're *not* thieves!' she began.

'You be quiet, my lad!' the first keeper snapped at her, he too thinking she was a boy. 'Let your big brother here do the talking! Carry on, young man, we're listening,' he said, turning to Julian, who was obviously the eldest.

Julian swallowed. 'My cousin Georgina is telling you the truth, sir,' he said. 'We – we're not thieves.'

The man cast a surprised glance at George.

'Oho – so she's a girl, is she? Very funny, I'm sure! Go on, young man!'

'We – we were just trying to catch a monkey – that one!'

In his confusion, poor Julian was getting his explanations all tangled up, and making matters worse. He looked and sounded guiltier than ever!

'Oh, so you admit it?' cried the keeper. 'You *are* trying to steal one of our animals.'

The man already had a firm grip on Julian's

74

arm. Poor Julian felt most uncomfortable.

'Well, you can explain the rest of it to the police!' said the keeper.

George hastily tried to explain, herself.

'Oh no – you don't understand!' she said. 'The monkey we're trying to catch doesn't belong to the zoo. It's ours – or at least, it's Tinker's. That's my friend here! Look at the monkey, and you'll see he's smaller than the others. That's how he managed to squeeze through the bars of the cage! He ran away from us, and Tinker was trying to catch him again, that's all – honestly!'

The two keepers obviously didn't believe a word of what George was telling them. The first man said sarcastically, 'Well, if he's your monkey, I'm sure he'll come if you call!'

'The fact is . . .' muttered Tinker. 'Well – look! Those other monkeys are all crowding round him and chattering away, and he can't even hear me. *And* he's found a friend who's holding him round the neck and won't let go – look!'

'Oh, don't let a little thing like that bother you!' said the keeper, still sounding sarcastic. 'We'll get the pair of 'em out of the cage, and *then* we'll soon see if one of them knows you!'

He went off to get two leather collars with leads on them, opened the door of the cage, and caught Mischief and the other monkey. Then he put the collars round their necks. Holding the leads, he told Tinker, 'Go on, then – call your monkey!'

This time, disturbed in the middle of his game, the frightened Mischief asked nothing better than to take refuge in Tinker's arms when the boy held them out to him. So at Tinker's call of 'Mischief'!' he made straight for his master. Unfortunately, his new friend imitated him a split second later – he too made for Tinker, who found himself with *two* monkeys in his arms!

Despite the fix they were in, George and her cousins couldn't help laughing. And in a moment the two keepers were laughing too.

'Not going to claim *both* monkeys belong to you, are you?' the first keeper inquired.

'No, sir,' said Tinker. 'Mine's the little one.'

'Prove it!'

Seeing that Tinker was at a loss, George had an idea.

'Listen!' she said. 'I suppose you know how many monkeys you keep in this cage? Well, all you have to do is count them. And if you find there's one too many, then you'll just *have* to believe us!'

Still laughing, the keeper did as she suggested. Sure enough, he found that there were thirteen monkeys in the cage. It usually held fourteen – so counting Mischief and his friend, the number of monkeys at the moment came to fifteen.

'Well, well, you win!' the keeper said, admitting that he was wrong with a good grace. 'As it seems this really is your monkey, you'd better take him home. But if the little rascal plays any more tricks, come knocking on my door another time, instead of breaking into the zoo without permission. You can see what that kind of thing leads to!'

'Oh, thank you, sir!' said Tinker, relieved.

'Come on, Mischief, let's go home.'

The keepers took off the collars and put the other monkey back in the cage. The children went off. Anne was waiting anxiously for them outside the fence. Sadly, Tinker told her that he hadn't found Attila – and he'd nearly lost Mischief too!

'What are we going to do now?' he said, sighing. 'How are we *ever* to find Attila? Any more ideas, George?'

'Yes!' said the intrepid George. 'We'll go on searching the countryside, and if we don't find anything by Thursday – well, I've got another plan in reserve for Thursday!'

Chapter Ten

GEORGE'S PLAN

Late on Wednesday afternoon, the Five and Tinker were holding a council of war in the field behind Big Hollow House. They were looking very serious. They had been patiently searching the countryside all round the house, but there was no denying that all their efforts to find Attila had ended in failure.

Tinker, lying on his front beside the stream, buried his face in the grass. 'We'll never, never find him,' he told the others, his voice muffled. 'And it shouldn't be all *that* easy to hide a cheetah!'

George threw away the blade of grass she had been chewing.

'Don't give up hope yet, Tinker,' she said. 'Remember I told you I had a last-ditch plan for tomorrow, if we hadn't found Attila by then?'

'In that case,' said Julian, 'it's about time you told us what it is! Personally, I just can't see what else we *could* do!'

George drew her knees up, rested her chin on

them, and looked at the others with a very determined expression on her face. All of them, Timmy included, were watching her expectantly.

'Luckily,' she said, 'we're left almost entirely to our own devices here at Big Hollow! So let's take advantage of our freedom and keep watch *very* late tomorrow – all night if necessary! Jenny thinks Attila is as good as dead already, and she'd never dream that we were trying to get on the track of his kidnappers. Your father's probably forgotten about the whole thing by now, Tinker. We're free to act, so let's take action!'

Dick looked at his cousin rather doubtfully.

'Hm,' he remarked. 'It strikes me that that's all we've been doing for days on end – taking action!'

'Yes, but in the dark, without any clues to guide us. Tomorrow it will be different!'

Julian, Dick, Anne and Tinker clamoured for more explanations. Where did George want them to keep watch? Instead of replying, George stood up, glancing at the time.

'Follow me!' she said. 'We can still get there by bike, and be back in time for dinner. I'll tell you my plan on the very spot!'

'*What* spot? Where is it? Where are you taking us?' asked Dick.

'To Little Hollow. It's the nearest seaside place to the beach where the kidnappers and their cocker spaniel came ashore. Come on, hurry up!'

The bicycle ride along the clifftop road was not a very long one. The children and Timmy passed the place they had started calling Spaniel's Beach, and the two bays farther down the coast next to it, and arrived at the fishing village of Little Hollow.

As soon as they got off their bikes, Julian, Dick, Anne and Tinker looked round in surprise. The village, usually such a quiet, sleepy sort of place, was buzzing like a beehive. There were men up ladders hanging decorations across the little streets. Women were draping decorated fishing nets over the harbour wall, and fishermen were scrubbing down their boats, which had little flags hung all over them.

'What's going on?' Anne wondered.

'They're getting ready for the village fête – actually, it's called a regatta, because part of it takes place on the water,' said George. 'It's to be held tomorrow afternoon and evening. That means that there'll be a lot going on here just when Tinker goes to the clearing to take the kidnappers his reply. There'll be boats with flags and bright lights cruising around the bay, and lots of visitors come to join in the fun. They're going to finish the regatta with a firework display.'

'I still don't see what use this regatta is to *us*,' said Julian.

'Don't you? Well, listen to me!'

Tinker interrupted George.

'I don't know what you're planning, George, but I can tell you one thing – I'm not going to steal my father's formula, and I'm not going to give it to those crooks. It's just too bad about – about Attila!'

His voice shook. George patted him kindly on the back.

'Don't be silly, old Tinker!' she said. Then, leading her companions to a quiet corner down by the jetty, where no one could hear what they said, she went on, 'My plan is quite simple really. Tomorrow evening, Tinker, you go to the clearing in Bluebell Wood on your own, at the time they say. You put a message in the wicker cage –'

'What sort of message?'

'A letter explaining that you're more than ready to do as the kidnappers say, if it means getting your pet back. Write, "I've tried to get hold of my father's formula, but I haven't managed to do it yet. I'm just waiting for a good moment. Give me a little more time, and as soon as I've got the formula I'll hang a scarf out of my bedroom window, and you can tell me where to hand the formula over –" '

'But they'll never agree!' groaned Tinker.

'That doesn't matter! You'll soon see why. And while you're taking your reply to the wood –'

'But what do I do after I've left it in the cage?' Tinker interrupted.

'You go home to Big Hollow House, and don't worry about anything! You musn't even try to look over your shoulder. Understand?'

'All right. But what about the rest of you?'

'Well, this is the clever part of my plan! *We'll* have been here in the village for several hours. And well before ten o'clock we'll have gone to

81

keep watch on the beach where the spaniel led Timmy before!'

Four pairs of eyes looked at George in surprise and admiration. 'Oh, I see!' Dick cried. 'We'll see the kidnappers arrive, with their dog – then the dog goes off to fetch the wicker cage, and we see him come back, and –'

'And all that leads us absolutely nowhere!' said Julian gloomily. 'That beach is flat as a pancake, remember? There's nowhere for us to hide. Anyway, how could we shadow the kidnappers? They'll set off again by sea, and our legs won't be much good then – nor will our bicycles!'

'I'm sure George has thought of that!' said Tinker confidently. 'Haven't you, George?'

George smiled, pleased to think her friend trusted her so much.

'Yes, I have,' she replied. 'I've thought of everything. We're going to hire a little motor boat. I did think of using your rowing boat *Bobabout!*, Tinker – the one we used for going out to the Demon's Rocks lighthouse at high tide – but I realised it wouldn't be fast enough. In a boat, we can easily go off and watch any part of the coast we like, pretending we're just having fun at the regatta. The comings and goings of so many other boats will give us cover. No one will notice us in the crowd! The kidnappers will be able to move about easily too, of course, but they won't have the faintest idea we're watching them!'

'Well done, George! That's a brilliant idea!'

Dick started to dance a little jig on the jetty! Several of the fishermen saw him, looked

Old Joe gave the children all sorts of good advice!

amused, and came over. Timmy was prancing around Dick too, and Tinker, excited at the prospect of getting his beloved Attila back, joined in the dance as well.

George and Julian, the practical ones, took advantage of this moment to strike up a conversation with the fishermen. They arranged to hire a little boat with an outboard motor for the next evening. At first the man who owned it wasn't sure about hiring it to a party of children, but Julian, who was big and strong for his age, and very responsible, promised that it would be all right with them. So the fisherman, Old Joe, agreed – giving the chidren all sorts of good advice!

When the Five and Tinker set off back along the road to Big Hollow, they were singing at the tops of their voices. They were in high spirits again! It didn't seem possible that this new plan of George's could lead them nowhere. There was so much in favour of it – at last, at long last, luck was on their side!

Chapter Eleven

THE REGATTA

Next day, the Five said goodbye to Tinker in the middle of the afternoon, reminding him of what he had to do.

'You're sure you remember?' asked George, for about the tenth time. 'You reach the clearing in Bluebell Wood at ten o'clock exactly. You leave the message there in the wicker cage, and you come *straight* back here without even turning round.'

'All *right*!' snapped Tinker, who was not all that keen on the prospect of going into the dark wood all by himself! 'All right, I get it! I'm not deaf or stupid, you know!'

His friends left, and set off for Little Hollow under a cloudless sky.

'Now we pretend to be ordinary visitors!' said Dick, when they had arrived. 'Let's go and leave our bikes with Old Joe the fisherman, and then we'll stroll round the village. Maybe Timmy will pick up a scent somewhere . . .'

So the Five went off to see Old Joe. They had

paid him a deposit for hiring his motor boat the day before, and now they gave him the rest of the money.

'You'll find *The Sprite* moored just off the jetty at eight o'clock,' the fisherman told the children. 'All you have to do is take her, and mind you look after her – I'm trusting you, young man!' he said to Julian.

The Five walked around the village. The fête was in full swing by now, but they did not see anyone who looked suspicous.

To pass the time and cheer themselves up, the children decided to have a go on the sideshows and rides, and they ended by enjoying themselves like everyone else. There were swingboats, shooting ranges, lucky dips, candy floss stalls, dodgem cars – they had a really good time!

About seven, though, Julian reminded them what they had really come for.

'I think we'd better go and have a bite to eat in that little snack bar,' he said. 'We must keep our strength up. Don't forget, there's adventure ahead of us – and we shall probably have to keep watch for quite a long time.'

George and her cousins were really hungry. They ate platefuls of sausages and chips and decided that slices of chocolate cake would help them to keep their strength up too! They washed it all down with fizzy lemonade, and finished their meal with strawberry and vanilla ice creams. Timmy wasn't forgotten, either – a kind woman behind the counter found him a nice big ham bone.

At last, looking at her watch, George said it was time to start.

'Let's go down to the jetty!'

'If we fall in the water now,' said Dick, laughing, 'we'll sink straight to the bottom, we're so full! I bet I weigh tons more than I did this morning!'

The Five found *The Sprite* just where Old Joe had said they would. She was quite an old rowing boat really, but she had a new little outboard motor fitted. The children got in, followed by Timmy, who was used to going anywhere and everywhere with George. George, who had lived by the sea all her life and prided herself on being able to handle all sorts of boats, took over the command. She examined the motor, made sure there was plenty of fuel, and then started up. The motor sprang to life. The boat quivered, and then shot off. George steered her steadily along, cruising in and out among the other boats, mostly still lying at anchor with all their flags and decorations ready. She wanted to get really used to the feel of *The Sprite* so that she could manoeuvre the boat quickly. She wasn't leaving anything to chance!

Soon afterwards, the fun spread down to the water's edge, and the regatta part of the fête began. The decorated boats started cruising round the bay to the sound of the cheerful music.

'There are going to be boat races soon,' said George. 'What a lot of people! Well, we can certainly cruise around without being afraid anyone will notice us.'

The Sprite herself was hung with pretty flags which flapped about in the wind. As they went along the children met other people enjoying themselves in boats. There was a great deal of coming and going, just as George had said. So the Five reached Spaniel's Beach by sea without arousing any curiosity at all!

Just inside the bay, they found a fairly sheltered spot. 'Let's anchor here,' said Julian. 'We've got a view of most of the beach, and the sea around us too.'

There was a rusty old anchor in the boat. Dick threw it into the water – its chain grated as he paid it out. George had switched off the motor. *The Sprite* stayed there, swaying gently on the waves. The children settled down in the dark to wait . . .

At first, time seemed to go quite fast. They could see the lights over in Little Hollow harbour, they heard the distant sound of music, and they watched the passing boats cruising up and down on the water. Whenever a boat came near them, flying flags and playing music, they wondered hopefully if it contained the kidnappers and their cocker spaniel. Their hearts beat faster – was it coming in to land there?

But they were disappointed every time. The boat always turned away again, and the children looked at each other gloomily. Suddenly the big clock on Little Hollow church tower struck ten, slowly. Ten o'clock – the time for Tinker to go to the clearing! And the kidnappers hadn't even turned up yet!

'Tinker must be reaching the clearing at this

very moment,' said Julian, under his breath. 'He'll be putting his letter in the wicker cage!'

'No, he won't because the cage won't be there!' cried Anne. 'The kidnappers have let him down.'

George looked at her cousins. She was very upset.

'I'm terribly afraid they must have put their wicker cage in the clearing before we even got here! Perhaps they went by road this time – or else they came ashore at a different place. Oh, how *silly* of me not to think of that before!'

Dick sighed.

'Even if you had, George, what could we have done about it? We couldn't possibly have kept watch on *all* the roads and every inch of the coastline! Your idea was very clever, but –'

'But the kidnappers were even cleverer!' finished George, in a toneless voice.

Anne took her hand gently.

'You did your best,' she said softly. 'Tinker won't hold it against you. He can't!'

'No – but I'm afraid this means a death sentence for poor Attila!'

The Five waited patiently for another whole hour, just in case, but nothing happened. The boat races in Little Hollow harbour were over now, and the firework display was lighting up the sky. Music rose into the air again.

'Let's go home,' said Julian. 'There's no point in catching our deaths of cold, waiting here any longer! I think the mist's already coming down.'

Sadly, the children returned *The Sprite* to Old Joc, who was waiting for them on the jetty, smoking his pipe. Then they retrieved their bicycles and set off back to Big Hollow House.

As they went along the road to Big Hollow, they had to pass Bluebell Wood, and suddenly George said, 'Do you mind if we stop a moment? I'd like to have a quick look at that clearing.'

Julian said he would go with her. While Dick and Anne guarded the bikes, the two cousins went in among the trees, with Timmy at their heels. They soon reached the clearing. Of course, the tree stump was still there – but there was no wicker cage on it.

'So the kidnappers never came to the meeting place!' said Julian.

'Yes, they did – they've been and gone!' said George. 'I mean, if Tinker *hadn't* found the cage here, he'd have left his message on the tree stump itself. That's the only thing he could have done!'

'Yes, you're right. Oh, blow! I suppose, as you said just now, the crooks didn't come by sea – or at least, not the same way as before!'

So Timmy wasn't the only one who had his tail between his legs when the Five got back to Big Hollow House, just after midnight. Naturally, Tinker wasn't asleep – he hadn't even gone to bed. George and her cousins found him in the garden, pacing up and down the path and waiting for them to get back.

'Well?' he whispered, seeing them slip into the quiet garden. 'Did you manage to follow the kidnappers? Do you know where Attila is? I left my letter in the wicker cage, so –'

He stopped suddenly, because he could tell from the other children's faces that their attempt had failed yet again! Their enemies, who were obviously very clever indeed, had outwitted them!

Chapter Twelve

A BRILLIANT IDEA!

Tinker and the Five hadn't expected to sleep well, but in fact they slept like logs until morning. They were so worn out that they simply dropped off, in spite of their disappointment and all their worries. Jenny had to call them several times before they finally got up and came down to breakfast.

'Whatever is the matter with you?' asked the housekeeper, serving scrambled eggs. 'I never saw such lazy children – why, it's nearly ten o'clock!'

Dear old Jenny had no idea how late the children had gone to bed the night before!

The weather was still very fine, but they spent a gloomy day, playing very quiet games without much enthusiasm. Jenny was quite worried to see their long faces, pale cheeks and dark-rimmed eyes at dinner time. She confronted them, her hands on her hips.

'Just look at you!' she said, sounding really concerned. 'What *is* the matter?'

'Nothing, nothing at all,' said Professor Hayling absent-mindedly. He thought Jenny was talking to *him*! 'Quite the opposite! I've very nearly finished copying out my formula, ready to be sent off to the Government!'

And he happily put the salt cellar in his pocket, left his glasses on the table beside the pepper pot, and went off to his study.

The children went out into the garden, where they organised a kind of circus on the lawn, with Timmy and Mischief as the star turns. But their hearts weren't in the game. A little later the postman came to the gate, with the day's second postal delivery, and saw the children.

'Hallo, young Tinker!' he called cheerily. 'Here's a letter for you!'

Smiling, he gave Tinker the letter, and then went off, whistling. Tinker glanced at the envelope and uttered an explanation.

'It – it's from *them*!' he stammered, eyes very wide. 'They're writing to me again!'

George, Julian, Dick and Anne looked at the envelope too. Yes, there was no doubt about it! Tinker was holding yet another letter from the kidnappers.

'Well, come on, Tinker! Quick, read it!'

Tinker hastily did as Dick had asked. He tore open the envelope, took out a rather crumpled sheet of paper, and read it out loud:

' "We hope that you really have been doing your best to get hold of the formula, but we can't give you much more time. This is the last you will be hearing from us. If you haven't brought the formula in three days' time, you'll never see your cheetah again. So come to the clearing in Bluebell Wood at ten o'clock on Monday evening. And don't push another letter or anything else like that in the wicker cage – all we want to find there is the formula, nothing else, and if we don't . . ." '

Tinker stopped, and swallowed hard.

'That's the end of the letter!' he said. 'There are only a few dots after that "if we don't".'

'And we know what *that* means!' said Dick glumly. 'Well, there's no way you can get out of it this time, old man. Either you let them have the formula, which is out of the question, or it's goodbye to poor Attila for ever.'

Tinker was very upset.

'I'll never see Attila again,' he whispered.

Anne, who was very tender-hearted, dissolved into tears. All these emotional upheavals were just too much for her. Tinker felt like following her example. As for Julian, he was gazing at George, who seemed to be deep in thought. Obviously her brain was working feverishly.

No one said anything for some time. Anne went on sobbing quietly, but no one tried to comfort her. The three boys, motionless, were *all* staring at George now, as if waiting for an oracle to speak! They were quite sure that her lively mind would think of *something* – something to give them hope again.

Sure enough, after a while George's brow cleared, and she even smiled at the others. Then, looking at her companions' long faces, she said in a teasing tone of voice, 'Well, while there's life there's hope! And Attila isn't dead yet, not as far as I know!'

'What do you mean, George?' cried Tinker. 'You've got an idea, haven't you?'

'Yes, I have! And I flatter myself it's a good idea, too! Mind you, it's a very daring one – but I think it's well worth trying!'

'Well, don't keep us in suspense!' said Julian.

'Tell us!' Dick begged his cousin. 'What *have* you thought of?'

'Something that's really very simple! Listen – we're going to carry the war into the enemy's camp. Since we can't seem to catch the kidnappers in the act, we'll give up any hope of that –'

'Is *that* your great idea?' asked Dick, disappointed. 'Giving up?'

'Do let me finish what I'm saying! This is going to be a case of tit for tat! The crooks who kidnapped your cheetah are about to find they've got competition, Tinker. We'll set up as kidnappers ourselves! On Monday, we'll go off with their cocker spaniel!'

You'd have thought a bomb had just exploded at the children's feet! Julian, Dick and Tinker – and even Anne, who had stopped crying – looked at George with their jaws dropping open.

They could hardly believe their ears!

'You're planning to *kidnap* the cocker spaniel?' repeated Julian.

'That's right! We can't get hold of the kidnappers themselves, but we *will* get hold of their dog. And we won't give him back – not until they give us Attila!'

'But – but a dog isn't worth as much as a cheetah,' Anne objected.

'Not in the normal way, no,' George agreed. 'But you see, *this* dog is a very special one. The kidnappers must have spent ages and taken no end of trouble to train him to fetch and carry for them. He must be invaluable to crooks who don't want to be seen themselves! I shouldn't be surprised if they really treasure that spaniel – and they must know he's far more use to them than your pet, Tinker. I mean, *think* of all he can do!'

Tinker's eyes were bright with hope again.

'You're right, George. But if we bring off the kidnapping, how do we get in touch with the dog's masters?'

'You're forgetting they want you to leave the formula in the wicker cage, Tinker. Well – instead of the formula, we'll leave an ultimatum addressed to the owners of the black spaniel. Attila or their dog!'

Tinker, Julian, Dick and Anne were much impressed by George's idea. They all started working out a detailed plan of action for Monday evening. Obviously it wouldn't be exactly easy to capture the cocker spaniel. The main difficulty was that they must lie in wait for him without letting him pick up their scent.

'We'll have to find which way the wind is blowing, and hide so that it doesn't carry our scent towards him,' said Julian. 'Then we must decide how to catch him –'

'I've thought of that,' said George. 'As soon as the black spaniel – oh, why don't we give him a name? I know – let's call him Pirate. Well, as soon as Pirate gets near the cage, Timmy must jump out at him!'

'You mean you're going to bring Timmy into it?' Tinker asked.

'Why not? He's one of the Five, isn't he? And he's better equipped than the rest of us for this part of the plan. Dog against dog – that's fair, isn't it?'

Julian looked doubtful.

'Well, Timmy's certainly bigger and faster than the span ... than Pirate! But you never know. We have to think of everything, and if Pirate gets away we'll be back where we started.'

'*I've* got an idea now!' cried Dick. 'If we want to make quite sure our plan works, let's catch the dog in a net. I mean a real net – a fishing net! I'm sure Old Joe would lend us one. He was pleased that we'd been so careful with his boat. As soon as Timmy has jumped out at Pirate, we'll throw the net over both dogs – and then we'll have Pirate in a trap!'

'Good idea, Dick! Well done!' said George. 'Now, Tinker, let's get that letter to the kidnappers written!'

A few minutes later Tinker was sitting at his desk, his tongue sticking out to help him concentrate, writing the letter his friends dictated to him. After making at least a dozen rough drafts, he copied the finished version out neatly and put it in an envelope.

Once this job was done, the children felt their spirits reviving. They couldn't be sad for too long! Next morning they got on their bicycles and rode off to Little Hollow to borrow a net from Old Joe. He was pleased to see them, and even invited them to go out fishing with him in *The Sprite*. They had great fun. It was a really holiday-like sort of day – the first one they seemed to have had for ages.

Chapter Thirteen

PIRATE

Saturday and Sunday passed, and nothing much happened. The children were waiting impatiently for Monday evening, with mingled hope and fear!

At last the time came. Soon after supper, the four cousins and Tinker set off along the coastal road. They took Timmy, of course, but not Mischief, in case he proved to live up to his name! The children hid their bicycles among some bushes just outside the wood. Then, leaving Tinker there, the Five made their way to the clearing in silence. The wicker cage was in its place. They could just make it out in the darkness.

Julian estimated which way the wind was blowing, and pointed out the best places for them to hide.

'I think that's the way Pirate will be coming, so he won't get wind of us here. Now, you wait just here, Dick, and whatever you do don't let go of your end of the fishing net. I'll hang on to the

99

other end. Jump out of hiding when I say so, and not before – understand? George, you try to make sure Timmy knows just what you want him to do!'

At ten o'clock precisely, Tinker arrived and put his message inside the wicker cage.

When the boy had gone again, the Five stayed perfectly still. George was grasping Timmy's collar. She was taut as a bowstring. Timmy could feel how tense she was – he realised they expected him to do something, but what was it? He didn't know *that* yet – and he wouldn't, until George pointed to the other dog and called, 'Go on, Timmy, get him!'

For the moment, however, Timmy remained alert and expectant, with all his senses at the ready – especially his keen senses of smell and hearing.

As for Julian and Dick, they were lurking in the shadows, waiting. In their minds, they were going over exactly what they'd have to do a moment or so later. They must stand up at just the same moment, co-ordinating their movements as they spread the net and dropped it over the two scuffling dogs. Anne was crouching behind a bramble bush a little way off.

Suddenly Timmy pricked up his ears. George stiffened. Anne suppressed a squeal of alarm. Her brothers' eyes turned to the spot where they had heard a faint crack of twigs. The sound came again, more clearly this time – and the black cocker spaniel appeared!

George bit her lip. Her hand clenched on

Timmy's collar, and she had to force herself not to move too soon.

The black spaniel sniffed the wind. Not smelling anything suspicious, he ran towards the tree stump. He opened his mouth to grasp the ring on top of the cage, and –

'Go on, Timmy – *get him*!'

George's shout was like a trumpet call! As if galvanised into life, Timmy bounded forward. *Now* he knew what his little mistress wanted him to do! He had to get the other dog by the scruff of the neck and throw him on the ground.

The black spaniel had raised his head in surprise. Seeing Timmy careering towards him, he realised he was in danger. Losing all interest in the cage, he jumped down off the stump, knocking the cage itself over, and tried to run for it. But he was too late! Timmy was on him already. The spaniel bravely turned to face his attacker, baring his teeth. Clever Timmy swerved and then attacked again. But the cocker spaniel was a brave dog. Finally, however, Tim managed to get him down on the ground, and soon poor Pirate was struggling under the bigger dog's weight.

Perhaps he might have escaped after all, by wriggling away, if Dick and Julian hadn't come to Timmy's aid. They rushed up to the two fighting dogs and flung Old Joe's net over them both. Caught in the fishing net, the surprised dogs stopped fighting of their own accord – and anyway, George was shouting, 'That's enough, Timmy – leave him! Wait a minute, old boy, and

101

we'll soon set you free. Gently, you boys – get Timmy out without letting Pirate escape. There, Timmy – good dog! Come on!'

Rather bewildered, Timmy obeyed. Then the boys got hold of the black spaniel, who let out a plaintive yelp. However, he didn't try to bite them.

Anne came out of her hiding place. Timid as she usually was, she suddenly wasn't at all frightened any more. She put out her hand to pat the black spaniel's nose.

'Oh, poor Pirate!' she said softly. 'You don't look nasty at all.'

The dog looked at her with big, soulful eyes, and licked her hand by way of answer. Happily, Anne patted him in a reassuring way, while Dick tied a piece of stout string to his collar.

'You're right, Anne,' said George. 'He certainly doesn't *look* vicious. I'm sure he'll follow us without much difficulty. Here, good dog – have a sugar lump! And here's one for you too, Timmy! Right – now be friends, both of you!'

Timmy came up to his adversary, wagging his tail. Pirate looked suspiciously at him, sniffed him, and then, guessing he had no more to fear now, let out a happy yelp.

'And now,' said Julian, putting back the overturned wicker cage, 'all we have to do is go back to Tinker – and wait to hear from the kidnappers! When Pirate doesn't turn up, they're bound to come to see what's happened and find Tinker's letter.'

They rushed up to the two fighting dogs and flung Old Joe's net over them both.

Anne patted him in a reassuring way.

103

'I'd love to see their faces when they read it!' said Dick, laughing. 'We've told them we won't set Pirate free until Attila's back at Big Hollow. Hooray for the Five! No one can fool around with *us* for long!'

'Let's just hope the plan works!' said Anne, with a sigh.

'Hurry up!' said George, bringing up the rear of the procession. 'We don't want to hang about here!'

Dick, who was holding Pirate on his makeshift leash, suddenly stopped.

'Why not? Why don't we stay and wait for the kidnappers? Then we could follow them!'

'Don't be silly! Pirate would bark and give us away, and *then* we'd be in a nice fix! Come on, that's enough talking. Off we go!'

The Five went back to Tinker, who was delighted and very relieved to see them and Pirate.

'Oh, marvellous! You got him! What do we do next?'

It was now that the children suddenly realised they had forgotten one very important point as they made their plans! Busy as they were thinking of the best way to capture Pirate, they had quite forgotten that they'd have to find somewhere to *hide* him while they negotiated with the kidnappers. Tinker's question showed what a big gap they had left in their preparations. They looked at each other, crestfallen.

'Oh, blow!' exclaimed Dick. 'Where *can* we take Pirate? Certainly not to your house, Tinker.

That's the first place the kidnappers would think of!'

'What's more,' Tinker added, 'Jenny would be very surprised to see him, and she'd ask all sorts of awkward questions!'

'All the same,' said Julian, 'we don't want to hide him too far from Big Hollow House, or it won't be very easy to go and feed him.'

'Oh dear,' said George gloomily. 'We ought to have thought of all this before! But we must find some sort of hiding place, and fast! Maybe there's a deserted fisherman's hut somewhere that would do?'

'Don't be silly,' said Dick. 'Anyone might come along and find him there, and set him free!'

'Suppose we tied him up in the very middle of the wood?' suggested Tinker. 'Somewhere nobody ever goes? We'd make a shelter for him, and come to visit him and feed him.'

'He'd be bored to death, you can bet, and then he'd bark!' Julian objected. 'No, we can't leave him all alone. His barking would soon be heard.'

It was an awkward problem. The children stood there on the outskirts of the wood with the two dogs, looking at each other and frowning. They'd thought they had scored such a triumph, and now it seemed as if one small detail might ruin everything!

Suddenly Tinker clapped his hands with delight.

'Oh, wonderful!' he cried. 'Simply wonderful! Why on earth didn't I think of it before? Yes, that's the answer!'

The others looked at him hopefully.

'*What's* the answer?' asked Dick. 'Do you know a good hiding place, Tinker?'

'I should just think I do! The best possible hiding place, in fact! There's no danger that Pirate will escape or be heard barking, and no one would think of looking for him there!'

'*Where*, for goodness' sake?' asked George impatiently.

'In my lighthouse, of course!'

George's face lit up.

'Oh yes – that really is a splendid idea!'

'I told you so!' said Tinker proudly. 'A *brilliant* idea! We'll go there straight away!'

Julian damped down his companions' enthusiasm.

'Wait a moment – Tinker, are you *sure* the lighthouse is safe? It does look more dilapidated than ever.'

Tinker looked annoyed. 'I told you! People thought it had been damaged, and now the villagers of Demon's Rocks and Little Hollow won't go near it, but don't worry! It's not in ruins, and it won't fall down on top of us, or on top of Pirate.'

Julian still didn't seem really convinced, so Tinker told his friends more about the architect, a friend of Professor Hayling, who had looked at the lighthouse for them. 'Dad may be absent-minded but he's no fool!' said Tinker. 'And he knew I'd be likely to slip off to play in my lighthouse whether he said I could or not! So he asked this architect what he thought.'

'And what *did* he think?' asked Julian.

'Well, he looked at all the stone masonry, and he measured the place up and down and backwards and forwards and sideways, and had a good look at the foundations too. Finally he said we'd all be dead and gone long before that lighthouse lost its first tooth – I mean its first stone! After that he had a good dinner with us, and while we were eating, Dad, who'd quite forgotten asking his friend in the first place, said it was nice to see him, but what exactly had brought him our way?'

Julian, Dick, Anne and George burst out laughing. Obviously Professor Hayling was never going to get any less absent-minded!

'All right!' said George, when she had finished laughing. 'In that case, I vote we take Pirate to the lighthouse!'

'Not this evening, though,' Julian advised them. 'It's too late, and it would be too dark out at Demon's Rocks. We'll hide the spaniel at Big Hollow just for tonight, and tomorrow, in secret, we'll all take your rowing boat to the lighthouse, Tinker.'

'We can't leave poor Pirate there all on his own,' said kind Anne. 'He'd feel so lost and lonely! And who knows – he might manage to swim ashore and escape!'

'We'll leave Timmy in charge of him,' George decided. 'I hate parting from my dog, but it shouldn't be for more than a day or two. Just until they give us back Attila!'

Chapter Fourteen

THE LIGHTHOUSE AGAIN

Now they had decided on a hiding place for Pirate, the children set off back home with both the dogs. Dick was still holding Pirate's makeshift leash.

They didn't sleep much that night. They were afraid the kidnappers might try doing something in revenge for the capture of their dog. George insisted on having Pirate in her room. She tied him to the foot of her bed – but first she gave him a really delicious meal. The cocker spaniel was feeling quite friendly towards Timmy now, though Timmy, feeling very responsible, kept a sharp eye on him. That wasn't very difficult, because Pirate did not seem to want to escape.

'Timmy, I'm counting on you to wake us if you hear the slightest suspicious noise outside,' George told her dog.

'Woof!' Timmy reassured her.

All the same George hardly closed her eyes till morning.

It was quite a complicated business getting

over to the lighthouse after breakfast. For one thing, the children didn't want Jenny to see them leaving with the cocker spaniel. (Professor Hayling didn't count. *He* could have seen them leave the house with three camels and an elephant, and he wouldn't have thought anything of it!) For another thing, and most important of all, they mustn't let the kidnappers spot them.

It was Anne who found the answer to the problem.

'Let's pretend we're going out to Demon's Rocks for a picnic in your lighthouse, Tinker,' she said. 'We'll hide Pirate in a big basket, cover him up with a tablecloth, and nobody will guess there's anything odd – unless he barks, of course!'

'He won't bark,' George assured her. 'I'll give him such a big breakfast that all he'll want to do is go to sleep in the basket. I've noticed what a greedy dog he is, and I think he's rather lazy too!'

Half an hour later, the children, Timmy and Mischief went down to the little jetty where Tinker's rowing boat *Bob-about!* was moored. Julian and Dick were carrying a basket with a tablecloth on top, and it looked just like a picnic basket. Tinker had stuffed the real picnic things into two haversacks – they were taking tomato sandwiches, hard-boiled eggs, fruit cake and apples. The children were talking rather loudly, for the benefit of anyone who might be eavesdropping, saying what they intended to do that day.

'It'll be such fun playing in your lighthouse,

Tinker! And we can have a real feast with all this delicious food we're taking over. Do hurry up and untie the boat!'

The children were in a hurry. They could hardly wait to moor the boat among the rocks behind the old lighthouse, and then scramble round to the steps in front, which led into the lighthouse itself. Once safely inside, it wouldn't matter any more even if Pirate did wake up and feel like barking.

The short crossing was easy. It was high tide, and Tinker skilfully brought the little boat over from the shore and in among the rocks. Then everyone jumped out. Dick, who was tired of carrying the spaniel, got him out of the basket. Pirate gave him a reproachful look, and then yawned and shook himself.

George and Tinker were already at the lighthouse door. Its rather rusty iron handle turned with difficulty, but at last they got it open and went inside.

'Hooray!' cried Tinker. 'Here we are at –'

A savage growling noise cut him short He stopped in amazement. George and Timmy stood perfectly still, and Julian, Anne and Dick – who was dragging Pirate along – hurried to join them.

'Whatever is it?' gasped Anne.

A second growl, even worse than the first one, set echoes ringing down the spiral staircase which ran through the middle of the lighthouse. 'GRRRRR!'

Tinker skilfully brought the little boat over from the shore.

'What luck we found him!' cried Dick

111

Tinker, getting over his fright, soon realised what it was.

'It – it can't be possible, but it *is*!' he murmured. 'It really does sound like – Attila!'

At that moment what looked like a torrential stream of black and yellow fur seemed to flow round the bend in the spiral staircase and down the stairs, landing at the boy's feet. Next moment Attila – for it really *was* the Haylings' tame cheetah – jumped up and put both front paws on Tinker's shoulders. Tinker sat down rather suddenly!

He had hardly recovered from his surprise when the cheetah tried to lick his face affectionately – but he couldn't. Poor Attila had a muzzle fastened over his nose and mouth.

Tinker got up at once and took the muzzle off. 'Attila, old boy!' he cried. 'So they were hiding you in my lighthouse the whole time! Who'd ever have guessed it?'

'Look,' said Anne. 'He's been tied up. There's a rope trailing along behind him – he must have broken it when he heard us!'

'What luck we found him!' cried Dick.

'Oh, I'm so glad!' said George, while Tim and Mischief greeted Attila with obvious pleasure. 'And see how well he's looking! The kidnappers can't have been starving him after all!'

Julian was the only one who was still worried. 'We'd better hurry up and get out of here,' he said. 'There's no time for dawdling! Do you realise that we've walked straight in to the lion's den? Or perhaps I should say, the cheetah's den! The kidnappers decided to hide in this lighthouse, because they thought no one came here any more – but they may come back any moment!' Lowering his voice, he added, 'Or they may even be here all the time!'

'Not likely,' said Dick. 'We didn't see any boat but our own, did we?'

'That doesn't prove anything,' Julian whispered. 'We know there's more than one of them, so one crook might be here while his friend or friends are on the mainland.'

'Well, let's search the lighthouse,' said George boldly. 'What with all of us, and Timmy, and Attila, it would be a funny thing if we couldn't cope with a single crook!'

Without listening to Julian's protests, Tinker, followed by the cheetah, was already on his way up to the top of the lighthouse. Suddenly his friends saw him running down the stairs again, very fast, looking pale and upset.

'The kidnappers!' he gasped, his voice shaking. 'I saw them coming from the gallery up there at the top! They're on board a big motor launch – oh, what shall we do? They must be quite close by now, and we can't possibly get away. Anyway, we only have a rowing boat, and they'd soon catch us!'

'I did warn you!' said Julian, in dismay. 'Well, it's too late to try escaping now.'

'Oh dear, whatever will become of us?' moaned Anne softly.

'Blow! Blow and bother!' said George. 'There must be *some* way – listen, our boat is very small, and we moored it around behind the lighthouse, where it's well hidden. The kidnappers won't see it when they arrive, so they won't suspect we're here.'

'But they're going to *find* us here all right!' said Julian gloomily. 'There's nowhere we can hide from them – specially not with this menagerie! If we take shelter in one of the upstairs rooms they'll have us in a trap. This staircase winds right up through the building!'

'Then let's go up it!' cried George.

Her companions looked at her blankly.

'Up it?' said Dick. 'But the staircase ends in the lamp-room at the very top. You weren't intending to dive off the tower into the sea, were you? Ju's right – if we climb up there we'll be trapped.'

'Yes, of course – *if* the kidnappers follow us up. But why should they? If you ask me, they'll be quite content to stay in the room down at the bottom. They'll think Attila is still tied up where they left him, upstairs. Anyway, my idea's worth trying, and we'd better get a move on! Follow me! I can hear the engine of their boat.'

George started racing up the spiral staircase, and as there really wasn't much choice, the others followed her. The children went round several bends in the spiral staircase. Dick had picked Pirate up, and was talking to him in a soothing voice, hoping against hope that the spaniel wouldn't start to bark. But the dog, who had a placid nature, was too pleased to have someone petting him to bother about barking. He closed his eyes and let Dick rock him like a baby!

The children soon came to a little landing. There was a cupboard on their right, with its door swinging open. They saw some ropes and a grappling hook inside it. A narrow window like a loophole with bars over it looked out over the sea.

'I wonder why they built bars into the windows of this lighthouse?' said Julian.

'To make things easier for people who want to tie up kidnapped cheetahs!' said George, pointing to a broken cord with its end trailing on the floor. 'This must be where they were keeping Attila, Tinker!'

The sound of the main door to the lighthouse opening below them interrupted George. They all froze and listened. George thumped Tinker on the back.

'Tie Attila up again and put his muzzle back on!' she whispered.

'Don't be an ass! Attila can defend us if necessary.'

'Oh, don't argue, just do as I tell you – and quick!'

Puzzled, Tinker obeyed her. The muzzle was still hanging round Attila's neck, and he put it back in place. Hastily, he tied the big cat up.

'Now, let's climb on!' said George under her breath. 'Tim, Mischief – keep quiet! Dick – you make sure Pirate doesn't bark and give us all away.'

Chapter Fifteen

THE KIDNAPPERS

Like shadows, the children, the dogs and the monkey made their way up about twenty more steps, leaving Attila there on the landing.

'But *why*?' Anne whispered.

'Ssh! Here they come!'

And so they did. The children heard men's heavy footsteps climbing the stairs. Anne was trembling with fright. If the men came on, past the landing . . . But that was where they stopped.

'Here – there's some meat, you filthy brute!' said a loud voice, obviously addressing the cheetah. 'You'll have to manage as best you can with your muzzle on – I'm not risking you snapping my hand off!'

'Listen, Gus,' said another voice, 'we've had this blinking animal on our hands long enough! Let's take him back where we found him, wait for those kids to give Tommy back, and then clear out – we'd better give up the notion of getting hold of that formula!'

'You must be raving, Vic! Don't you know that piece of paper's worth a fortune to us?'

The children heard the man called Vic speaking again. He was almost whining!

'And it could mean years in jail, Gus, you know that as well as I do!'

'We'll be in far more danger of jail if we let that cheetah go! Then those infernal kids who fooled us last night by going off with Tommy will follow the dog when he makes his way back to us – and that'll give us away!'

Hearing his masters talking, Pirate, otherwise Tommy, opened one eye and waggled an ear. But Dick hugged him gently, George popped a sugar lump into his mouth, and the dog remained blissfully quiet!

The crooks' voices suddenly died away as their footsteps rang out on the iron staircase again. They were going back down! The children looked at each other in relief, almost smiling. As if they understood, Timmy wagged his tail and Mischief started pulling Tinker's hair.

'Good! They're going away,' Dick whispered.

'But only down to the room at the bottom of the lighthouse,' George whispered back. 'Come on, let's go down too. We need to know how they plan to get hold of your father's formula now, Tinker!' And she had already climbed down several stairs, going ahead of the others, when she heard one of the crooks coming up again! Taken by surprise, George just had time to slip into the cupboard containing the ropes. She pulled the door nearly shut, and crouched there in the dark. Above her, the other children held their breath in suspense. Dick had only just managed to stop Pirate dashing down after her.

Through the slight gap in the cupboard doorway, George saw a man with a very hangdog look pass her. He bent down, picked up a packet of cigarettes which he must have dropped on the landing floor, and then turned away again. George waited for him to join his friend before she came out of hiding. She called up to the others in a low voice, 'Come on – all clear! You can untie Attila and take his muzzle off again Tinker!'

All together, the little group began cautiously climbing downstairs.

'What are we going to do now?' Dick asked in a low voice.

'Try to get away, of course!' said George in the same tone. 'Watch out – here's the last bend in the stairs.'

She slowed down, craning her neck. The two men had gone into the downstairs room, but unfortunately for the children, they hadn't shut the door behind them. They could be heard talking loudly.

'If I had that Hayling lad there, and those friends of his, I'd wring the necks of the whole bunch!' growled Gus.

'And no more than they deserve,' said Vic. 'I suppose those wretched kids think they're clever, kidnapping our dog and leaving us a note like that. I nearly had a heart attack when you read it out!'

'Well, they'll soon be sorry! They'll wish they never took *me* on at my own game! I'm not returning that cheetah, and we'll get Tommy back too, *and* the Professor's formula. I have a plan. Only we can't stay here – you heard what they said over in the village? The barometer's going down, and there's a big storm brewing up. We don't want to wait for this old ruin of a lighthouse to come crashing round our ears. We'll go to ground somewhere else! So you go up and fetch that cheetah, Vic.'

The children trembled. If the men came up, they were done for – and there was no time to retrace their steps now! But luckily Vic and Gus were still talking, down below.

'You're crazy!' Vic was saying. 'If we take that cheetah out of here in broad daylight, everyone will be able to see us!'

'No, they won't!' Gus retorted. 'They won't stop to look at us – with that gale warning out, the fishermen will either be safe indoors at home, or busy mooring their boats securely. They'll all be busy. That's why we were able to come back here just now without bothering to hide too much!'

'All the same, it's risky!'

'So is staying here! I tell you, we're short of time!'

George guessed that Gus would win the argument with his accomplice, and the two men might come out of the big room any moment now.

'Oh, if only they'd closed the door behind

them!' she breathed. 'We could have tiptoed past without a sound, got into our boat, and we'd have been far away before they realised what had become of Attila!'

But as it was, they couldn't possibly walk past the open door before the criminals' very eyes. The men would see them and grab them. They might be armed, and then – well, it was better not to imagine just *what* might happen then!

'I'm frightened,' Anne whispered, putting a trembling hand on her big brother's arm. 'Ju, I'm frightened!'

Julian clumsily tried to reassure her.

'Calm down, Anne. Everything will be all right!'

But anyone could tell he didn't believe a word of what he was saying. In fact, things had seldom looked so desperate to him as they did now. It was a gloomy outlook. The Five and Tinker hadn't been in such a tight corner as this during the whole adventure! The children knew they simply had to get away without losing any more time. The animals themselves were suddenly feeling nervous, and were on the alert. Even Pirate – the children still thought of him as Pirate and not Tommy – had wriggled until Dick put him down, and then huddled close to the boy's legs, quite quiet, not showing any wish to join his former masters. It was obvious he preferred to stay with his kidnappers! No doubt the two men hadn't treated their dog very well.

George herself couldn't think of anything to

do, for once in her life. She just didn't see *how* they were to get out of this fix.

And then Tinker had an idea.

'Wait a moment. I want to try something.'

Looking at him, the others wondered if he had suddenly gone mad. He crouched down on the stairs, with Mischief in front of him, and began making a series of such funny, ridiculous gestures that the monkey started to imitate him. Mischief was interested in this new game!

Tinker rubbed his nose. So did Mischief. Tinker scratched his neck. So did Mischief. And so on, and so on! Julian interrupted this performance.

'Are you nuts, or what? This is no time for – for monkey tricks!'

'Ssh!' said Tinker. 'It's going to work. Watch this!'

He had just shown Tinker the half-open door of a small store cupboard. Then, tiptoeing towards it, he quickly closed the door, and turned the key in the lock. After that he opened it again.

Julian, Dick, Anne and George watched. They had no idea what Tinker was trying to do at first, but light began to dawn when they saw Mischief, in his turn, make for the cupboard. Imitating everything Tinker did, he closed the cupboard door and turned the key.

He didn't bother to close it quietly, and the noise sounded very loud to the children, but just then there was a rumble of thunder outside which drowned all other sounds. The storm the two men had mentioned was breaking!

Tinker opened the door yet again, closed it, re-opened it, and showed it to Mischief. In his turn, the monkey happily closed the door and turned the key in the lock once more.

Beaming, Tinker turned to his friends. 'There, what do you think of that?' he asked.

'I'll tell you, if you really want to know,' snorted Julian. 'I think it's a waste of precious time! We could have got back upstairs by now!'

'But don't you see the idea?' Dick asked his brother.

'Of course I do. I'm not an idiot. But how do you expect Tinker to get Mischief to close the door of the *room* down there?'

Still pursuing his bright idea, Tinker was already opening the cupboard door again. Just for a moment, even Dick and George couldn't see where all this was leading.

But Mischief was getting more and more interested in the new game. He thought his young master had invented it specially to amuse him. He leaped forward to close the door and turn the key in the lock for the third time.

This time, however, Tinker wouldn't let him. He closed the door himself, leaned against it, and wouldn't allow the little monkey anywhere near it. Disappointed, Mischief started uttering plaintive little cries and trying to push Tinker away so that he could get at the cupboard door. But Tinker wouldn't budge an inch.

Instead, he pointed to the open door of the

room at the bottom of the stairs. George and her cousins hardly dared to breathe. Now – if only Mischief would understand Tinker's gesture, and go to close *that* door!

'Go on, Mischief!' Tinker whispered.

Chapter Sixteen

A DARING ESCAPE

Julian glanced at his watch. The second hand seemed to be simply racing round. Even if Mischief *did* decide to go and close the door, would he be in time?

It was certainly a good idea of Tinker's. Unfortunately, Julian thought, there wasn't much chance it would be successful. Julian was afraid the noise Mischief was making might attract the men's attention, and that was what Anne feared too. Luckily, Vic and Gus were still arguing.

And outside the storm became so violent all of a sudden that the roar of the wind and the crash of the waves drowned all the noises inside the lighthouse. Dick was wondering if their own little boat, moored among the rocks, would stand up to the breakers much longer. George was watching Mischief in suspense, hoping against hope that he'd understand what Tinker wanted him to do, and play his part.

Almost as if she were getting the message to

124

him by telepathy, Mischief suddenly seemed to get the idea. He looked at the open door at the foot of the stairs, and with one bound leaped down the last few steps. Then, chattering away and dancing about all the time, he went up to the door and pushed it as hard as he could – which wasn't *very* hard! The children watched in suspense. If Mischief didn't manage to close that door – if all he did was attract the attention of the men on the other side of it . . .

And closing the door wasn't all, either. He had to turn the key in the lock as well. The horrified children suddenly saw that the lock itself, with the key sticking out of it, was too high up for Mischief. He'd never be able to reach!

Suddenly the door responded to the little monkey's efforts, and swung shut with a bang. Mischief stood perfectly still in alarm, apparently forgetting about the key.

Anne closed her eyes. Any moment now the startled and angry men would rush out of their lair . . . But when nothing happened, she plucked up her courage and opened her eyes again.

She looked downstairs. At any other time, what she saw would have made her laugh!

Mischief, who had remembered that he was supposed to lock the door too, was jumping up and down trying to reach the key. Anne wondered why the closing of the door hadn't alerted the crooks, and then she realised that they must have thought a gust of wind had blown it shut. After all, there's nothing odd about a door slamming in the wind!

'What luck!' she thought. But then her fears were revived as she saw that the monkey's efforts to jump up to the key were all in vain. Worse still, furious at not being able to get at the key, Mischief began to squeak and gibber shrilly. Perhaps the noise of the storm might not be loud enough to cover the sound he was making after all.

'And *then* we'll be done for!' thought Anne.

At the same time, Dick whispered, 'Well, the door's shut, and that's what we wanted. Nothing venture, nothing win – so let's try getting out!'

The children and the animals went down the last few steps of the staircase as fast and as quietly as they could. As they were passing the door of the room, George had a sudden flash of inspiration. Why shouldn't *she* do what Mischief couldn't? If the crooks found they were locked in, well, they'd be angry, but there'd be nothing they could do about it – they wouldn't be able to pursue the children!

Acting on impulse, and with her usual daring, George took hold of the key and gently turned it in the lock. But the lock itself was rusty. Probably it wasn't often used – and as the key turned, it made a horrid grating sound. Just as there was sudden lull in the storm, too! The men must surely have heard that noise.

This time the children didn't hesitate for a moment. They rushed out as fast as they possibly could, dragging Attila, Timmy, Mischief and Pirate after them.

Dick, bringing up the rear, felt his heart turn

over as he passed the door of the room. He saw the latch move, and then there was a chorus of oaths from inside the room! Finding themselves prisoners, the crooks began beating on the door with their fists.

'Quick!' Dick called to the others. 'They're trying to break the door down. We must hurry!'

The little boat *Bob-about!* was tied up behind the lighthouse, and to reach it the children had to pass the windows of the room where the crooks were imprisoned. They couldn't help glancing in. The man George had seen on the landing inside the lighthouse was grasping the bars of one of the windows, shaking them furiously.

'Never mind that door, Vic!' he shouted to his friend, who was still banging on the door. 'Come and help me work this bar loose instead. It's beginning to move. If I could get my hands on whoever done this, I'd –'

Suddenly he caught sight of the children and his eyes nearly popped out of his head!

'Those kids!' he yelled. 'It's them! And they're making their getaway – with the cheetah, too!'

Vic was at the window in a flash.

'It's them all right!' he said. 'Well, blow me! They've got Tommy as well!'

Gus's face went red as a lobster. He looked so fierce that Anne let out a cry of alarm. 'Oh, suppose they catch up with us!'

Gus and Vic, swallowing their rage for the time being, had grabbed the bars of the window and were tugging at them as hard as they could. It looked as if they'd be free in a few moments – free to follow the children! Then the whole adventure would come to a sticky end!

Julian raced for the rocks behind the lighthouse, urging the others on. Once they reached the rocks, the children saw a sight which was thrilling and terrifying at the same time. Only a little way out, the sea was covered with huge, white-crested waves. Soon these vast waves would be breaking against the rocks – and would crush their fragile little boat unless they got away in time. It was even more urgent to escape now!

'Quick, get aboard!' cried Tinker.

Dick pushed his little sister Anne into the boat, and the others jumped in too, with the animals. The boat was just big enough to take them all, but it was a squash. The rain beat down, whipping at the waves, and flashes of lightning darted through the dark clouds. Thunder was rumbling all round them.

George and Julian took the oars.

'Don't worry!' George yelled into the wind. 'We'll make it all right! The main thing is to get round the lighthouse as fast as we can – it'll be calmer on the other side.'

Anne's teeth were chattering. 'But those men have a motor-boat,' she reminded the others. 'They'll soon catch up with us!'

George managed to smile, even though she was pulling at the oars with all her might.

'Don't fuss, Anne!' she shouted. 'I've got an

idea. The kidnappers haven't caught up with us yet – but we must hurry if my plan's to succeed! Come on, Julian, row!'

The boat rounded the lighthouse, with some difficulty. *Bob-about!* was shipping water the whole time, and was in danger of capsizing.

Attila was growling softly. His fur was wet, and he didn't like this one bit! Timmy was suffering in silence, but he never took his eyes off George. Pirate just sat there calmly. He trusted the children! Mischief was whimpering, with his face buried in his master's neck, and as for Dick and Tinker, they didn't say a word. They did not even dare to look at the lighthouse, afraid that they might see the crooks climbing out of the window if they did.

Julian and George, bent over the oars, were rowing as hard as they could. George had just one idea in her head.

'I only hope those shaky bars will hold just a little while longer,' she thought. 'Oh, I hope there's time for my plan to work.'

At last the little boat was on the side of the lighthouse facing the shore. As George had said, the water was not so rough here.

'Make for the jetty by the lighthouse steps, Julian!' George gasped. 'And fast!'

In his astonishment, Julian stopped rowing instead, and the boat turned round on its own axis and nearly capsized.

'Do as I say!' yelled George furiously. 'It's part of my plan – it's our only hope of safety!'

Julian gave up trying to make out why George wanted to go *back* to the lighthouse, instead of making for the safety of the mainland, and obeyed her. A moment later, their little boat was alongside the motor launch in which the crooks had arrived.

'Quick – all aboard their boat!' George told the others. 'Once we're in, I'll tie our own boat to the back!'

This time Julian, Dick, Anne and Tinker saw the idea – they were going to make their escape in the motor launch, leaving the crooks marooned!

It was quite easy for the children and animals to change over to the launch. In fact, the two boats, lying side by side, didn't move about very much because they were in the shelter of the calmer water. The only hard part was getting Attila to move into the bigger boat, but they did it as last. George herself was the last to get in. With Dick's help, she tied the rowing boat on behind them.

'Now, start the engine, Julian!'

She had only just shouted these words through the storm when Tinker and Anne cried out at the same moment, 'Look, here they come!'

Sure enough, the gesticulating figures of the two men had just appeared at the top of the steps. They were making for the boats and the children!

Julian made the engine roar, and the boat shot off, bounding over the waves and pulling the little rowing boat along. Just in time! The crooks were powerless now. All they could do was shake their fists at the children, but that was a futile gesture! The men were prisoners in Demon's Rocks lighthouse.

'We're safe!' cried Dick.

Chapter Seventeen

ATTILA IS HOME AGAIN!

But they weren't quite safe yet, after all. Once the motor launch was out of the patch of calm water, they found themselves among the rough waves again. Julian had never had much practice in handling a boat as big as this, and he found it quite difficult to turn the wheel and keep their course set for land. He had to take care not to turn sideways on to the big waves, or to ship too much water.

Sometimes the motor-boat was carried up on a big wave and then fell back, shaking horribly, with its framework creaking and groaning. The children just hoped it wouldn't break up entirely.

Suddenly, George and Tinker both saw that the painter tying the rowing boat to the launch was coming adrift. They moved to tighten the knot at the same time. George's haste made her careless. She leaned a long way out over the side to re-tie the rope, and before she had time to get properly back in the launch again, it rose up on another huge wave and fell back with amazing violence. It was so sudden that George didn't even have time to clutch hold of anything. She plunged overboard head first and disappeared into the foaming water.

Anne screamed.

'Julian, stop! George has fallen in – she'll drown!'

It wasn't easy to steer the boat at all in such heavy seas, but Julian managed to make it go round in a big circle. As it did, the rowing boat, still pulled along behind, passed quite close to George, who was thrashing about in the water. She didn't lose her head, but caught hold of the little boat and scrambled into it as nimbly as Mischief himself could have done.

She was gasping for air, had no breath left to speak. She could only wave to Julian, to let him know she was all right, and he was to go on.

The motor-boat set off for land again, leaping over the waves. George, alone in the rowing boat being towed along behind, was badly shaken, but she was still as brave as ever. She clenched her teeth to stop them chattering, although she couldn't help shivering. She had to hold on tight the whole time, so as not to be thrown out into the water again – she knew she was too tired to be able to swim now! She hardly had the strength even to cling to the boat.

Meanwhile, on board the motor launch, Dick, Tinker and Anne were having trouble with Timmy. No sooner did the brave dog see his mistress in danger than he had prepared to leap into the water himself, and now, unable to bear being apart from her, he was trying to jump into the rowing boat and join her. As soon as George had enough breath, she shouted as loud as she could, 'No, Timmy! Be good! Lie down – good dog!'

Tim heard her, and understood. He obeyed, though it went against the grain! That was just as well, because as soon as Dick, Tinker and Anne let go of him, all their efforts were needed for another task. The painter tying the two boats together looked like coming unhitched for the second time. And it would be more serious this time, because if it *did* come adrift, George would be in great danger.

'Help me!' cried Dick, grabbing the rope. 'Hang on to this, you two, and hold on! We musn't let go till we reach land.'

But that was easier said than done. The rough rope scorched the three children's hands, and every time the boat rocked they were in danger of letting go. Anne's hands were soon scraped and sore, but she still clung bravely and desperately to the rope, and didn't even wince.

George saw the danger she was in, and could tell how brave the others were being. There wasn't anything she could to do help but wait and hope!

But luckily they were not far from shore now. Soon, Julian could cut out the engine, and they came in to the little harbour of Demon's Rocks village. The village fishermen, who had seen the drama, had gone to put on their oilskins and sou'westers. The rain was running off them as they stood on the jetty, ready to put out to the rescue if necessary – but it wasn't necessary!

The two boats came ashore undamaged.

Julian, Dick, Tinker and Anne were the first to get out, hauling their menagerie after them. Then it was George's turn to land. She hugged the others.

When the fishermen saw the cheetah and the other animals, they were very surprised. 'My word, it looks like a circus!' said one of them.

The skipper of one of the fishing boats recognised Tinker.

'Why, that's young Tinker Hayling!' he said. 'Well, you've had a lucky escape, young man, and so have your friends here!'

Julian turned to him. Pointing to George, he said, 'Sir, if you wouldn't mind – my cousin fell into the water, and I'm afraid she may catch cold and be ill. She ought to get dry at once. In fact, we're all pretty wet – is there anywhere we could –'

But George interrupted him. She had wrapped herself in the oilskins one of the fishermen had kindly lent her, and she thought that would do. 'I'm not going anywhere except the police station!' she said. 'The main thing now is to get those crooks over in the lighthouse arrested – though I don't suppose they can get away!'

The skipper laughed. 'That they can't! No one would be able to swim over in seas like this – and the storm's going on a while yet!'

He was right. The children had time to get dry at the nearest police station while they told the whole story of their adventure. The sergeant on

duty there was very surprised, and kept interrupting them with exclamations of amazement.
When they had finished, he said, 'Well, well,
well! Sounds like you've done a good job there!
Gus and Vic – the Force has been looking for
those two this last two months!'

And the sergeant telephoned the police in the
nearest town. An important superintendent
there said he and several of his men would soon
arrive.

While they waited for the police reinforce-
ments, the children enjoyed mugs of hot cocoa
provided by the kindly sergeant. It was delicious,
with lots of creamy froth on top. Timmy,
Mischief and Pirate were dried and fed too – and
so was Attila, though Tinker put his muzzle back
on just for the moment, so that he wouldn't
frighten anyone.

When the superintendent arrived, the children
went over the whole story of the last few days
again for his benefit. He congratulated them
warmly.

'If the criminals we're about to arrest, thanks to
you, really are the men we've been after for so
long, the public will be much indebted to you
young people. Well, the storm's dying down, so
I'll get hold of a police boat and go out to that
lighthouse with my men.'

'Can we come too?' asked George, who was
never frightened of anything.

The superintendent laughed. 'No, you certainly can't! Those men may be armed, and
there's no point in having you run any *more* risks

– you've done quite enough of that as it is!' But then, seeing the children's disappointed faces, he added, 'However, if you take these fieldglasses you'll be able to watch us make the arrest. It'll be like having a ringside seat, which you certainly deserve!'

A few minutes later, when the storm had completely died down and the sun was out again, Tinker and the Five saw the policemen start out for the lighthouse.

'I do hope everything goes all right,' sighed Anne.

Everything went very much all right – and thanks to the fieldglasses, the children had a good view of the policemen getting out of their boat at the steps up to the lighthouse.

The crooks didn't put up any resistance.

'I can't see their faces too well,' said George, straining her eyes, 'but it looks as if they realise they're outnumbered.'

'*That'll* teach them to go kidnapping Attila!' said Tinker fiercely.

The police got back into their boat, with the prisoners. Over at Demon's Rocks village, the fishermen and the children were impatiently waiting for their return. When the boat came in, the superintendent made the two men come on land in front of him.

'Yes, these are the fellows we were after, all right!' he told the children. 'And thanks to you, they'll be spending quite a few years in prison!'

Attila growled ferociously at Gus and Vic, who passed him with doleful expressions on their faces and their wrists in handcuffs. Tinker had to calm him down.

'And tomorrow,' the superintendent added, 'we'll be asking you to come to the city police station to make an official statement. I hope you won't mind doing that. I'm afraid,' he added, smiling, 'you may find there are rather a lot of press reporters pestering you, so you'd better be prepared to see your pictures in the papers!'

The children laughed happily – they didn't mind that, now that everything was over. Suddenly, Tinker asked, 'Do you think we can keep Pirate? That's the criminals' dog. He hasn't got a master now, and he seems to have made friends with my cheetah and my monkey. I'd like to adopt him.'

'I should think that'll be all right. Well, we'll see you young people tomorrow!'

So all the children had to do now was go home to Big Hollow House. As soon as they arrived, Tinker rushed into the kitchen.

'Hallo, Jenny!' he said. 'We're back!'

'Oh, thank goodness!' said Jenny. 'I was really worried about you, over at Demon's Rocks in that storm!'

'And we've brought someone else back with us,' Tinker went on, opening the door to let in Julian, Dick, Anne, George, Timmy, Pirate, Mischief and – the cheetah! 'Look who's here!'

At the sight of the big cat, Jenny exclaimed, 'Why, good gracious, it's Attila! Wherever did you find him, Tinker?'

'Up in the lighthouse – you can read all about it

in the papers tomorrow!'

'Can't you tell me now?'

'Not till we've got some food inside us, *please*, Jenny! We never had time for our picnic lunch, and we haven't eaten a thing since this morning. Nor have the animals – and that includes this spaniel. Attila and Mischief have adopted him! So if you don't want us to die of starvation ...'

But dear old Jenny was already laying out a splendid supper on the table. There was cold chicken and pork pie, with lettuce and tomatoes and newly-baked bread rolls, followed by a great big bowl of strawberries and cream, and ginger beer to drink. Tinker and his friends sat down to enjoy it.

'I do wonder what your father will say when he finds that Attila's back, Tinker!' said George happily.

At that very moment Professor Hayling came into the room.

'Goodness me,' he said, absent-mindedly. 'What have we here? A cheetah – now where on earth did you pick *that* up, Tinker? As if there weren't enough animals around this house already!'

And with these words the Professor turned and went out again, while the children dissolved into helpless laughter!

If you have enjoyed this book here are some more that you might like to read, also published by Knight Books:

NICHOLAS FISK

STARSTORMERS
SUNBURST
CATFANG
EVIL EYE
VOLCANO

Four children have escaped a tired, depleted Earth in a homemade spaceship. It is a desperate attempt to find their parents, who are working to establish a new settlement on a distant planet.

These exciting titles in the Starstormer Saga follow their nerve-racking adventures, alone in space, and their fight against the evil forces of the Octopus Emperor.

Three more adventures of the Famous Five,
told by Claude Voilier, translated by Anthea Bell:

THE FAMOUS FIVE AND THE STATELY HOMES GANG

Another holiday at Kirrin Cottage proves to be
as exciting as all the others from the moment
the Five set off on their shiny new bicycles!

THE FAMOUS FIVE AND THE MYSTERY OF THE EMERALDS

When George overhears a couple of crooks
planning a jewel robbery, the Famous Five
set off on a dangerous and thrilling trail.

THE FAMOUS FIVE GO ON TELEVISION

A holiday treat is even more exciting than
expected when the Five are invited to play
themselves in a television series.

KNIGHT BOOKS

A complete list of the FAMOUS FIVE
ADVENTURES by Enid Blyton:

KNIGHT BOOKS